MY ETERNAL SUNSHINE

YOU MAKE ME FEEL ALIVE

MORE SRIVIDYA

Dedicated to everyone facing tough times and finding the strength to keep going, may their lives be filled with beauty and hope.

Contents

Foreword vii

Preface ix

Acknowledgements xi

Prologue xiii

1. Chapter 1 1

2. Chapter 2 4

3. Chapter 3 10

4. Chapter 4 25

5. Chapter 5 37

6. Chapter 6 41

7. Chapter 7 46

8. Chapter 8 61

9. Chapter 9 75

10. Chapter 10 87

11. Chapter 11 98

12. Chapter 12 105

13. Chapter 13 116

14. Chapter 14 122

15. Chapter 15 128

16. Chapter 16 133

Foreword

"*Reviving eternal serendipity celebrates the unexpected beauty of finding love in the twilight of life, where every moment holds the promise of renewal and every embrace ignites the flame of everlasting devotion*"

Preface

As Ph.D. research scholar, my days are often consumed by the pursuit of academic excellence and scholarly endeavors. However, amidst the rigors of academia, there has always been a burning desire within me to venture into the realm of fiction.

For years, I harbored a dream of penning down a compelling story, one that would captivate readers and transport them to a world of imagination and wonder. Despite the demands of my daily life, I made a conscious decision to carve out time for my passion and embark on the journey of writing my debut novel.

With each word penned, I found solace and fulfillment in the creative process and experiences into the narrative tapestry of my story. As the characters of Surya and Lily came to life on the pages, I realized that fiction offered me a unique opportunity to explore themes of love, resilience, and human connection in a way that transcended the boundaries of academia.

Today, as I stand on the threshold of sharing my book with the world, I am filled with a profound sense of joy and gratitude. It is my sincerest hope that "My Eternal Sunshine" will resonate with readers, sparking their imagination and touching their hearts in ways that only fiction can.

I am immensely grateful for this opportunity to share my passion and my novel with you all. Happy reading.

Warm regards,

More Srividya

♥♥♥

Acknowledgements

I extend my heartfelt gratitude to my dear SRJ for unwavering support and encouragement throughout this journey. Your presence has been my guiding light, illuminating even the darkest moments with warmth and reassurance. My sunshine, thank you for being my constant source of inspiration and strength. I am also deeply grateful to my parents for their unwavering love, guidance, and sacrifices, which have shaped me into the person I am today.

Prologue

With her new keypad phone clutched tightly in her hand, Lily revealed in the newfound freedom of constant communication with Adi. Their conversations flowed effortlessly, meandering through topics both trivial and profound as they navigated the intricacies of their burgeoning relationship. From stolen moments stolen between classes to late-night chats that stretched into the early hours of dawn, Lily and Adi's connection seemed to deepen with each passing day.

But amidst the laughter and love, a shadow of uncertainty loomed on the horizon a question that lingered in the air like a whisper on the wind. And it was on one such weekend, as Lily bid Adi goodnight and retreated to the sanctuary of her hostel room, that the question finally surfaced, breaking through the surface of their idyllic romance like a stone thrown into a tranquil pond.

As Lily settled into her bed, her thoughts drifting like autumn leaves on a gentle breeze, her phone illuminated with a message from Adi. Her heart fluttered in her chest as she read his words, her eyes scanning the screen with a mixture of excitement and trepidation.

"Lily, I've been thinking... I really care about you, and I want to be closer to you in every way. Would you like to make love?"

The words hung in the air, heavy with the weight of their implications. For Lily, they sparked a whirlwind of emotions desire mingled with uncertainty, passion intertwined with fear. She felt her pulse quicken and her breath catch in her throat as she grappled with the enormity of Adi's request.

In that moment of silence, as she stared at the glowing screen of her phone, Lily felt a wave of conflicting emotions wash over her. On one hand, there was a part of her that longed to say yes to surrender herself completely to the man she loved, to explore the depths of their connection in the most intimate of ways. But on the other hand, there was a nagging voice in the back of her mind a voice filled with doubt and apprehension, whispering tales of uncertainty and fear.

She worried about what making love would mean for their relationship whether it would change the dynamic between them, whether it would bring them closer together or tear them apart. She worried about whether she was truly ready to take such a momentous step to expose herself so completely, body and soul, to another person.

And above all, she worried about what Adi would think of her response whether he would be disappointed or hurt if she couldn't find the courage to say yes, whether he would still love her just the same if she chose to say no.

In the midst of her turmoil, Lily felt a pang of guilt gnawing at her heart. She knew that Adi deserved an answer that he was baring his soul to her in a moment of vulnerability, and she owed him the same honesty and openness in return. But she couldn't bring herself to reply not yet, not until she had sorted through the maelstrom of emotions swirling within her.

And so, with a heavy heart and a mind in turmoil, Lily closed her eyes and let the weight of Adi's words wash over her like a tidal wave, knowing that whatever decision she made would shape the course of their relationship for better or for worse.

But just as she was lost in the tumult of her thoughts, her phone buzzed once again, pulling her back from the edge of uncertainty. With trembling hands, she opened the message from Adi, her heart pounding in her chest as she read his words.

"I'm sorry, Lily," he wrote. "There is no pressure. If you're not ready, we don't have to take things any further. Your feelings matter to me, and I only want what's best for you."

Tears welled up in Lily's eyes as she read Adi's words, touched by his sensitivity and understanding. In that moment, she realized just how much he truly cared for her, how deeply he respected her boundaries and her autonomy.

With a shaky breath and a heart full of love, Lily mustered up the courage to reply, her fingers trembling as she typed out her response.

"Yes, Adi," she wrote. "I want to be with you, in every way. Let's do it."

Adi replied "Thank you My love. Good night"

She replied back with "Good night"

As the night stretched on, Lily found herself engulfed in a whirlwind of thoughts and emotions. Despite the anticipation of what lay ahead with Adi, she couldn't shake off the nagging fears that crept into her mind. Happiness and excitement mingled with uncertainty and confusion, leaving her restless and unable to find solace in sleep.

With each passing moment, her mind raced with questions and doubts, casting shadows of doubt on the decisions she had made. Was she doing the right thing? Was this the path she truly wanted to tread? The conflicting emotions tugged at her heart, leaving her torn between the desire to embrace love and the fear of the unknown.

Yet amidst the uncertainty, one thing remained clear her love for Adi was unwavering. Despite the doubts that plagued her mind, she found comfort in the thought of being with him, of sharing this intimate moment together.

As she tossed and turned in bed, her thoughts flitting from one concern to the next, she couldn't help but wonder what the future held. But despite the uncertainty, a glimmer of hope remained a hope that whispered of love's transformative power, of the possibility of finding happiness amidst the turmoil of doubt.

"Lily is a resilient young woman who has overcome adversity with grace and determination. Her strength lies not only in her ability to weather life's storms but also in her unwavering optimism and capacity for love. With a heart as boundless as her dreams, Lily navigates life's twists and turns with courage and compassion, inspiring those around her with her unwavering spirit."

1

Seeking Love in the Shadows

Once upon a time, in a charming little village nestled amidst rolling hills and whispering streams, there dwelled a young girl named Lily. Despite the beauty that surrounded her, Lily's childhood was clouded by the constant arguments between her parents. Every day, she sought solace in the vast fields, gazing up at the endless sky, dreaming of a future where she could escape the turmoil and have a home of her own, where peace would reign supreme.

Lily was a cheerful and independent child, with dreams of financial freedom budding in her heart from a very tender age. School became her refuge, a place where she could immerse herself in learning and laughter, away from the tumultuous atmosphere at home. Though she was still young, Lily couldn't ignore the shadows of domestic violence that lurked in the corners of her mind.

In her small village school, Lily was a standout student, always striving to do her best in her studies. She dreamed of a brighter future, one that was different from her current life. Every day, as she went about her routines in the village, she couldn't help but feel a sense of longing for something more. The simple life around her contrasted sharply with her aspirations for something greater. It was as if she could see beyond the boundaries of her troubled home, envisioning a world where she could make her own choices and escape the difficulties of her past. This longing filled her with a mix of hope and determination, driving her to pursue her dreams no matter what obstacles lay in her path.

Since she was young, Lily felt a heavy burden in her heart, as if no one truly cared for her at home. She sought love and approval from others outside her family. Whenever relatives or neighbors showed her kindness, it lifted her spirits and made her feel loved. Their warm gestures helped soothe the pain she carried inside, offering a sense of comfort and belonging that was often missing in her own home. This longing for love and acceptance filled her with a deep sense of yearning, driving her to seek out connections with others who could offer her the affection and validation she craved.

Whenever an aunt patted her back or a neighbor waved hello, Lily's heart swelled with warmth and comfort. She longed for the love of a family that felt out of reach, so she cherished every fleeting moment of affection she received from others. These small acts of kindness reassured her that she was worthy of love and belonging, even if it came from unexpected sources. Each gesture, no matter how small, filled the void in her heart and gave her hope that one day, she would find the love and acceptance she yearned for.

Despite feeling deeply lonely, Lily remained strong, refusing to let the lack of love at home break her spirit. She reached out to others, treasuring every bit of kindness she received like a rare treasure in her harsh world.

In the faces of her relatives and neighbors, Lily glimpsed the love and acceptance she craved. Their small acts of kindness kept her going, offering a ray of hope in the darkness that surrounded her.

Despite the temporary nature of the love she found outside her home, it provided Lily with a glimmer of hope in her dark world. It reminded her that even in the midst of pain and loneliness, there was still kindness and warmth to be found.

As she grew older, Lily's dreams solidified into a clear vision of financial independence. She held onto the dream of having a home filled with laughter, where arguments would fade into the background. Lily's determination became her guiding light, and she devoted herself to her studies, seeing education as her ticket out of the shadows of her childhood.

With each passing day, Lily's resilience grew stronger, propelling her forward in pursuit of her goals. She clung to the belief that one day, she would create a life for herself far removed from the struggles of her upbringing.

2

Lily's Struggle with School Politics

When Lily reached the age of ten, a significant opportunity arose that had the potential to change her life. It came in the form of an invitation to attend a residential school. Just hearing about this chance filled Lily with a mix of emotions excitement, hope, and maybe a hint of fear. It was like a glimmer of light breaking through the darkness that surrounded her at home.

As the days drew nearer for Lily to leave, you could see the excitement sparkling in her eyes. She was filled with a bubbling feeling of anticipation, unlike the other kids who were sad to say goodbye to their families. Lily was eager to embark on this new adventure away from home.

As Lily packed her things into her suitcase, her mind buzzed with excitement about the fresh start ahead. The idea of entering a world of learning and freedom made her feel thrilled and almost as if she couldn't believe it was real. To Lily, the residential school meant more than just a chance to learn it was a way to escape from the difficult things that happened in her home.

As Lily packed bags and got ready to leave, her parents felt a mix of pride and worry. They weren't sure about letting her go, but they knew it was an important chance for her future.

On the day she left, Lily stood at the doorway, ready to begin a new part of her life. She felt a mix of excitement and nervousness in her heart. With every step towards the bus, she felt determined to make the most of this chance and create a future full of hope.

As the bus pulled away from the familiar streets of her village, Lily turned her gaze towards the horizon, her eyes alight with anticipation. For the first time in her young life, she felt a sense of freedom wash over her, a freedom born from the knowledge that she was finally taking control of her own destiny.

As the scenery disappeared from view, Lily smiled, feeling hopeful about the journey ahead. She knew that she was starting a new adventure that would bring her closer to a better future.

In the bustling halls of the residential school, Lily felt a sense of excitement and anticipation. She knew that amidst the new friendships and academic adventures, she would discover the courage to face any obstacles that came her way.

In Lily's school life, happiness became her constant companion. Her dedication to her studies and her bright intellect earned her admiration from both teachers and peers alike. With each passing day, she thrived in the nurturing environment of the school, her enthusiasm for learning shining through in every task she undertook.

Surrounded by good friends who shared her passion for education, Lily's days were filled with laughter and camaraderie. Together, they navigated the challenges of school life, supporting each other through thick and thin.

But amidst the familiarity of her routine, a new presence entered Lily's life one that would leave an indelible mark on her heart. A new teacher arrived, his arrival heralding a subtle shift in the fabric of Lily's world. From the moment she first set eyes on him, she felt drawn to his warmth and kindness, his unwavering support a beacon of encouragement in her academic journey.

As their interactions grew more frequent, Lily found herself looking forward to each encounter with eager anticipation. The new teacher's friendly demeanor and genuine interest in her well-being struck a chord within her, sparking a connection that transcended the boundaries of the classroom.

In his presence, Lily felt understood and valued in a way she had never experienced before. He saw beyond her academic achievements, recognizing the depth of her potential and encouraging her to reach for the stars.

Their bond grew stronger with each passing day, their conversations ranging from schoolwork to personal aspirations. In him, Lily found not only a mentor but also a confidant a guiding light who illuminated the path towards her dreams.

Amidst the challenges of growing up, Lily found solace and encouragement in the unwavering support of her biology teacher. His presence provided her with a sense of comfort and inspiration, guiding her through the ups and downs of adolescence. With him by her side, she felt empowered to overcome obstacles and pursue her dreams with confidence. In his classroom, she blossomed, her spirits lifted by his encouragement and belief in her abilities. Through his guidance, she discovered newfound strength and resilience, propelling her towards a future filled with hope and promise.

As puberty descended upon Lily and her peers like a storm cloud on the horizon, the innocence of childhood began to fade, replaced by the tumultuous whirlwind of adolescence. Amidst the changes and uncertainties, Lily found herself navigating a treacherous landscape fraught with pitfalls and obstacles.

It all began innocently enough a harmless crush on her biology teacher, whose passion for the subject ignited a spark within Lily's soul. She found herself drawn to his intellect, his passion, his warmth. But little did she know that this seemingly innocent infatuation would soon spiral into a maelstrom of chaos and confusion.

Lily's friends, caught up in the whirlwind of adolescent fantasies, began to confide in each other, sharing their secret crushes and whispered confessions. And unwittingly, Lily found herself swept up in the tide, her own feelings for her biology teacher consuming her thoughts and desires. In the school hallways, quiet talk floated around like ghostly whispers, spreading stories about secret feelings and hidden meetings between students and teachers. These rumors made the atmosphere feel heavy and mysterious, like something secretive and forbidden was happening. It stirred up strong emotions among the students, mixing curiosity with worry and fear. People felt unsure and uneasy, not knowing what was true and what wasn't. For students like Lily, caught in the middle of it all, it was a confusing and unsettling time, with emotions swirling like leaves in the wind.

But as the whispers grew louder and the rumors spread like wildfire, the school became a breeding ground for jealousy, resentment, and suspicion. The teachers, embroiled in their own petty rivalries and power struggles, turned a blind eye to the brewing storm, allowing favoritism and animosity to poison the atmosphere.

In the midst of the chaos, amid all the confusion, Lily got caught in a difficult situation where she became a part of a problem she didn't choose. The physics teacher, feeling jealous of his colleague's popularity and the students' admiration for him, started treating Lily badly. He blamed her for things she didn't do and made her feel ashamed. As rumors spread and people talked more, Lily felt like an outsider, rejected by her classmates and not understood by her teachers.

Feeling lonely and lost in a place where people were unfriendly and angry towards her, Lily felt like she was suffocating under the heavy weight of loneliness. She withdrew from others, becoming quieter and sadder than before. Tears filled her eyes often, and she cried silently, feeling upset and hopeless.

In the darkness of her despair, Lily began to question everything she once held dear. She doubted her worth, her value, her very existence. She felt unloved, unwanted, unworthy of the affection she so desperately craved. And as the days stretched into weeks and the weeks into months, she sank deeper and deeper into the abyss of her own despair.

In the middle of all the sadness, Lily found a tiny bit of hope, like a small light shining far away. Even though she was having a hard time, she found comfort in unexpected places: in the kindness of her seniors she didn't know, in the happiness of seeing someone smile, and in the friendly hugs from a friend.

Bit by bit, Lily started to recover from her tough situation. Even though things were hard, she didn't give up. Her strong will and bravery helped her get through the toughest times. As the secondary school board exams approached, she gathered all her strength and courage, determined to overcome the challenges and show everyone what she was capable of.

On the big day of exams, Lily was ready. With a strong determination, she tackled the questions, feeling confident despite all the challenges she had faced. And when the results came out, there she was, at the top of the list. It was a proud moment for her, a sign of all the hard work and strength she had shown. She stood tall, feeling proud of herself, knowing that she had overcome everything that had come her way.

Despite the joy and praise surrounding her achievements, Lily couldn't escape the lingering sadness from her school days. The farewell event, filled with smiles and goodbyes, didn't bring her any happiness. She couldn't confront the painful memories of betrayal and hurt that still troubled her. Those memories haunted her dreams, making it difficult for her to move on and fully enjoy the moment.

When it was time to say goodbye to her school, Lily decided to leave quietly, without any big goodbye. She left behind a place filled with sad memories and unfulfilled hopes, but she took with her the valuable lessons she learned, the friendships she made, and the inner strength she gained from facing challenges. She felt a mix of emotions as she walked away from the school grounds for the last time sadness for the difficult times she endured, but also a sense of pride for overcoming them and moving forward with her life.

3

Lily's first love

During summer vacation, Lily visited her aunt's house where she met a boy named Adi. Adi was the kind of person who could light up a room with just his smile. His charm and teasing nature made him a favorite. He had a knack for making people laugh, always ready with a witty remark or a playful joke. But beyond his playful exterior, Adi was incredibly caring. He had a heart of gold and would go out of his way to help those in need. From the moment their eyes met, there was an undeniable spark between them a magnetic pull that drew them together like moths to a flame. Adi possessed a charm that was as irresistible as it was enchanting, his every word and gesture leaving Lily spellbound.

Adi and Lily clicked instantly, spending time together exploring the surroundings, sharing laughter, and creating memories.

Adi's charming demeanor and friendly nature drew Lily closer to him, and soon they found themselves enjoying each other's company. Their bond grew stronger with each passing day, filling Lily's heart with happiness and excitement. Little did she know that this chance encounter would blossom into something beautiful, igniting a spark that would change the course of her life forever.

With a smile that could light up the darkest of nights, Adi wasted no time in showering Lily with attention, his playful banter and teasing glances igniting a fire within her soul. He was a master of flirtation, weaving a tapestry of sweet words and gentle touches that left Lily's heart racing with excitement.

Though she was no stranger to the ways of the world, Lily found herself entranced by Adi's allure, swept away by the whirlwind of emotions that enveloped her in his presence. She understood the game he played, the delicate dance of attraction and desire, yet she couldn't help but revel in the happiness he brought into her life.

Every moment spent with Adi was a treasure to be cherished, a symphony of laughter and joy that echoed through the halls of her aunt's home. He had a way of making her feel alive, of seeing the beauty within her that she had long forgotten existed.

But amidst the heady rush of newfound love, Lily remained grounded in reality, mindful of the fleeting nature of summer romances. She knew that their time together was limited, that soon she would have to return to the confines of her everyday life, leaving behind the warmth of Adi's embrace.

In the gentle embrace of a summer evening, as the golden rays of the sun danced across the horizon, Adi gathered his courage and poured out his heart to Lily. With trembling hands and a nervous smile, he professed his love, leaving Lily at a loss for words. She stood there, her heart pounding with a mixture of disbelief and joy, unable to comprehend the depth of emotion swelling within her chest. But despite her initial shock, there was no denying the happiness that bubbled up inside her. For in Adi's declaration of love, Lily found a warmth and tenderness unlike anything she had ever known.

From that moment on, Adi became a constant presence in Lily's life, his caring nature and playful antics bringing a sense of lightness to her days. He treated her with a tenderness that touched her soul, his gestures of affection leaving her feeling cherished and adored. And with each passing day, Lily found herself falling deeper and deeper under his spell, unable to resist the magnetic pull of his love.

One day, when the house was empty and the world seemed to stand still, Adi pulled Lily into his arms and pressed a gentle kiss to her cheek. It was a simple gesture, but it sent a thrill of electricity coursing through her veins, leaving her breathless with emotion. In that moment, Lily knew that she was experiencing a love unlike any other a love that filled her with an overwhelming sense of happiness and contentment.

But as quickly as their blissful days together had begun, they were soon interrupted by the harsh reality of life. Lily received news that she had been accepted into a prestigious pre-university college, a dream she had long harbored in her heart. Despite her excitement at the prospect of furthering her education, Lily couldn't shake the pang of sadness that gripped her heart at the thought of leaving Adi behind.

With no phone to communicate with him, Lily felt the weight of their separation bearing down on her like a heavy burden. She longed for Adi's presence, his comforting words and loving embrace, to soothe the ache of loneliness that gnawed at her soul. Each passing day without him felt like an eternity, and Lily found herself counting down the moments until they could be reunited once more.

But even in the midst of her longing, Lily threw herself into her studies with renewed determination. Surrounded by classmates who admired her talents and dedication, she found solace in the bustling atmosphere of the college hostel. And though the distance between her and Adi remained a constant ache in her heart, Lily drew strength from the knowledge that their love would endure, no matter the miles that separated them.

Each day became a struggle for Lily, her heart heavy with the weight of longing. Adi had become her everything, the light that brightened even the darkest corners of her world. His absence left a void within her, a longing that could not be quenched by anything else.

But despite the challenges they faced, Lily clung to the hope that one day, their love would triumph over all obstacles. With each passing moment, her resolve strengthened, fueling her determination to find a way to be with Adi, no matter the cost.

As two long years drifted by, Lily's heart ached with the absence of Adi by her side. Their meetings had become few and far between, fleeting moments stolen amidst the bustling crowds of festivals, where the watchful eyes of family and parents stood as barriers between them. Unable to exchange more than a passing glance, Lily yearned for the chance to hold Adi close and pour out the depths of her love to him.

Finally, the day arrived when Lily's pre-university college journey came to an end. With her heart set on a new beginning, she eagerly awaited news of her admission to the university. And when the acceptance letter arrived, her joy knew no bounds.

For Lily had been granted admission to the very university where Adi lived a twist of fate that felt like a gift from the heavens above. With tears of happiness streaming down her cheeks, Lily knew that this was her chance to be near the love of her life, to finally bridge the gap that had kept them apart for so long.

With a heart full of hope and anticipation, Lily wasted no time in enrolling in the university. She took up residence in the hostel, eager to immerse herself in this new chapter of her life. And as she settled into her new surroundings, she was greeted by two roommates who would soon become her closest confidantes and lifelong friends.

Together, they embarked on this journey of discovery, navigating the ups and downs of university life with laughter and camaraderie. Lily found solace in the companionship of her roommates, their support serving as a pillar of strength as she awaited the moment when she would finally be reunited with Adi.

In the busy city streets, amidst the chaos and clamor of everyday life, Lily found solace in the arms of Adi, her beloved companion and steadfast confidant. With each passing weekend, their love blossomed like a delicate flower, unfurling its petals to reveal the depths of their affection for one another.

Adi, with his infectious smile and playful demeanor, swept Lily off her feet from the moment they met. His bike became their chariot, whisking them away on adventures that spanned every corner of the city. As Lily nestled herself against his back, feeling the warmth of his body and the steady rhythm of his heartbeat, she knew that she was exactly where she belonged.

With each ride, Adi's hands would find Lily's, guiding her to hold on tightly as they navigated the bustling streets together. The simple act of intertwining their fingers filled Lily with a sense of security and belonging, as though nothing in the world could ever tear them apart.

Their weekends were a whirlwind of laughter and joy, spent exploring the city's myriad attractions hand in hand. From shopping malls to parks, they revealed in each other's company, savouring the precious moments they shared together. Adi's declarations of love echoed in Lily's ears like a sweet melody, filling her heart with a sense of happiness that knew no bounds.

"I love you forever and ever," Adi would whisper in her ear, his words like music to her soul. "I never ever want to leave you. You are my everything."

With each proclamation of love, Lily's heart soared, her love for Adi growing stronger with each passing day. She found herself unable to express the depths of her affection in words, her love for him transcending language and logic. Instead, she poured her heart out in simple gestures a bouquet of flowers, a colorful balloon symbols of her undying devotion to the man who had captured her heart.

Together, they embarked on a journey of discovery, exploring the hidden gems and secret treasures that lay hidden within the city's embrace. From quaint cafes to bustling markets, they savored every moment they spent together, creating memories that would last a lifetime.

But amidst the laughter and joy, Lily knew that their time together was precious and fleeting. Without Adi by her side, she felt adrift in a sea of uncertainty, her love for him anchoring her to the present moment. For in his arms, she found a sense of peace and contentment that she had never known before.

As Lily's college days unfurled like the pages of a cherished novel, each chapter brought with it a kaleidoscope of emotions and experiences. From the thrill of new friendships to the excitement of academic pursuits, her days were filled with a vibrant tapestry of learning and growth. And woven into the fabric of her everyday life was the love she shared with Adi a love that danced like a flame in the darkness, casting its warm glow upon her heart.

With her new keypad phone clutched tightly in her hand, Lily revealed in the newfound freedom of constant communication with Adi. Their conversations flowed effortlessly, meandering through topics both trivial and profound as they navigated the intricacies of their burgeoning relationship. From stolen moments stolen between classes to late-night chats that stretched into the early hours of dawn, Lily and Adi's connection seemed to deepen with each passing day.

But amidst the laughter and love, a shadow of uncertainty loomed on the horizon a question that lingered in the air like a whisper on the wind. And it was on one such weekend, as Lily bid Adi goodnight and retreated to the sanctuary of her hostel room, that the question finally surfaced, breaking through the surface of their idyllic romance like a stone thrown into a tranquil pond.

As Lily settled into her bed, her thoughts drifting like autumn leaves on a gentle breeze, her phone illuminated with a message from Adi. Her heart fluttered in her chest as she read his words, her eyes scanning the screen with a mixture of excitement and trepidation.

"Lily, I've been thinking... I really care about you, and I want to be closer to you in every way. Would you like to make love?"

The words hung in the air, heavy with the weight of their implications. For Lily, they sparked a whirlwind of emotions desire mingled with uncertainty, passion intertwined with fear. She felt her pulse quicken and her breath catch in her throat as she grappled with the enormity of Adi's request.

In that moment of silence, as she stared at the glowing screen of her phone, Lily felt a wave of conflicting emotions wash over her. On one hand, there was a part of her that longed to say yes to surrender herself completely to the man she loved, to explore the depths of their connection in the most intimate of ways. But on the other hand, there was a nagging voice in the back of her mind a voice filled with doubt and apprehension, whispering tales of uncertainty and fear.

She worried about what making love would mean for their relationship whether it would change the dynamic between them, whether it would bring them closer together or tear them apart. She worried about whether she was truly ready to take such a momentous step to expose herself so completely, body and soul, to another person.

And above all, she worried about what Adi would think of her response whether he would be disappointed or hurt if she couldn't find the courage to say yes, whether he would still love her just the same if she chose to say no.

In the midst of her turmoil, Lily felt a pang of guilt gnawing at her heart. She knew that Adi deserved an answer that he was baring his soul to her in a moment of vulnerability, and she owed him the same honesty and openness in return. But she couldn't bring herself to reply not yet, not until she had sorted through the maelstrom of emotions swirling within her.

And so, with a heavy heart and a mind in turmoil, Lily closed her eyes and let the weight of Adi's words wash over her like a tidal wave, knowing that whatever decision she made would shape the course of their relationship for better or for worse.

But just as she was lost in the tumult of her thoughts, her phone buzzed once again, pulling her back from the edge of uncertainty. With trembling hands, she opened the message from Adi, her heart pounding in her chest as she read his words.

"I'm sorry, Lily," he wrote. "There is no pressure. If you're not ready, we don't have to take things any further. Your feelings matter to me, and I only want what's best for you."

Tears welled up in Lily's eyes as she read Adi's words, touched by his sensitivity and understanding. In that moment, she realized just how much he truly cared for her, how deeply he respected her boundaries and her autonomy.

With a shaky breath and a heart full of love, Lily mustered up the courage to reply, her fingers trembling as she typed out her response.

"Yes, Adi," she wrote. "I want to be with you, in every way. Let's do it."

Adi replied "Thank you My love. Good night"

She replied back with "Good night"

As the night stretched on, Lily found herself engulfed in a whirlwind of thoughts and emotions. Despite the anticipation of what lay ahead with Adi, she couldn't shake off the nagging fears that crept into her mind. Happiness and excitement mingled with uncertainty and confusion, leaving her restless and unable to find solace in sleep.

With each passing moment, her mind raced with questions and doubts, casting shadows of doubt on the decisions she had made. Was she doing the right thing? Was this the path she truly wanted to tread? The conflicting emotions tugged at her heart, leaving her torn between the desire to embrace love and the fear of the unknown.

Yet amidst the uncertainty, one thing remained clear her love for Adi was unwavering. Despite the doubts that plagued her mind, she found comfort in the thought of being with him, of sharing this intimate moment together.

As she tossed and turned in bed, her thoughts flitting from one concern to the next, she couldn't help but wonder what the future held. But despite the uncertainty, a glimmer of hope remained a hope that whispered of love's transformative power, of the possibility of finding happiness amidst the turmoil of doubt.

And so, as the night waned and the first light of dawn peeked through the curtains, Lily found herself caught in the delicate balance between fear and excitement, uncertainty and hope; a balance that would ultimately shape the course of her journey with Adi.

She trusted Adi with all her heart, but the thought of what lay ahead filled her with a myriad of fears and doubts. As the day approached, she found herself unable to sleep, her mind a whirlwind of conflicting emotions. Despite her fears, Lily knew one thing for certain her love for Adi surpassed all else. With him, she felt safe, cherished, and whole. And so, as they prepared to take this momentous step together, she pushed aside her doubts and fears, focusing instead on the love that bound them together.

On the weekend, Adi's uncle's family went on a trip, leaving the house empty. Seizing the opportunity, Adi invited Lily to join him. Excited for an adventure together, they embarked on a journey to Adi's uncle's vacation spot, ready to make cherished memories in each other's company.

In the quiet solitude of Adi's uncle's empty house, Lily's heart raced with a mixture of excitement and apprehension. As they entered the empty house, the silence enveloped them like a warm embrace, broken only by the sound of their beating hearts. Adi, ever the gentleman, made sure Lily felt comfortable and at ease, his gentle touch and reassuring words melting away her anxieties.

With tender kisses and whispered declarations of love, they embarked on a journey of intimacy and passion, each moment filled with a depth of emotion that words could scarcely describe. As they surrendered themselves to each other, Lily felt a sense of connection unlike anything she had ever experienced before a sense of being truly and wholly loved.

With each caress, each whispered endearment, Lily felt herself falling deeper and deeper into the abyss of love a love that consumed her, body and soul, leaving her breathless and exhilarated. And in the arms of the man she loved, she found solace, she found ecstasy, she found a love that knew no bounds.

As the night wore on and the darkness gave way to the soft light of dawn, Lily and Adi lay entwined in each other's arms, their bodies spent from the intensity of their lovemaking. But amidst the afterglow of passion, a sense of peace settled over them, a peace born of the knowledge that they had shared something sacred, something beautiful, something that would bind them together for eternity.

As the first light of dawn gently filtered through the curtains, Lily and Adi stirred from their peaceful slumber, reluctantly awakening to the realities of the day ahead. With a sense of regret, Lily realized that she needed to return to her hostel before time slipped away. Adi, ever the gentleman, offered to accompany her back, ensuring she reached her destination safely.

The journey back to the hostel was filled with a comfortable silence, punctuated only by the occasional exchange of glances and shy smiles between Lily and Adi. Despite the impending separation, their hearts remained intertwined, each cherishing the memories of the unforgettable day they had shared together.

Upon reaching the hostel, Adi bid Lily farewell with a warm embrace, his eyes shining with affection as he whispered words of gratitude and love. "Thank you," he murmured softly, "this was the best ever day you gave to me. I love you, Lily."

Lily's cheeks flushed with a rosy hue as she reciprocated Adi's sentiments, her heart brimming with happiness and contentment. "Love you too," she replied shyly, her voice barely above a whisper.

As Adi departed, leaving Lily standing in the doorway of the hostel, a sense of warmth enveloped her, filling her with a profound sense of joy. She replayed the events of the day in her mind, each moment etched vividly in her memory the laughter, the smiles, the gentle touches all precious treasures she held close to her heart.

Throughout the day, Lily found herself lost in a reverie, her thoughts drifting back to the special moments she had shared with Adi. With each recollection, her cheeks would flush anew, a telltale sign of the lingering blush that adorned her features.

Unbeknownst to her, her friends had taken notice of her flushed complexion and dreamy demeanor, their playful teasing drawing attention to her obvious state of bliss. "Looks like someone's got a secret admirer," they teased, their laughter ringing through the air.

Though embarrassed by their teasing, Lily couldn't help but smile, her heart swelling with affection for the boy who had captured her heart. Despite their playful jibes, she knew that her feelings for Adi were genuine, and that the memories they had created together would remain etched in her heart forever.

As the day drew to a close and Lily settled into bed, she found herself lost in a whirlwind of emotions gratitude for the love she had found, excitement for the future that lay ahead, and above all, a profound sense of contentment that could only come from knowing that she was loved, cherished, and adored.

Every weekend became a canvas upon which Lily and Adi painted their love story, each moment infused with tenderness, passion, and a profound sense of connection. In the quiet intimacy of Adi's uncle's empty house, they found solace in each other's arms, their love blossoming with each tender touch and whispered declaration of affection.

Every stolen moment, every stolen kiss served as a testament to the depth of their devotion, their hearts beating in perfect harmony as they surrendered themselves wholly to the intoxicating bliss of their love.

With each passing week, their love story unfolded like the petals of a delicate flower, blossoming in the warmth of their affection. In the quiet moments between breaths, they found meaning and purpose in each other's arms, their love growing stronger with each passing day.

Their intimate moments were a symphony of passion and desire, their bodies entwined in a dance of ecstasy as they surrendered themselves completely to the fire that burned between them. In the sweetness of their embrace, they found solace and fulfillment, their love igniting a flame that would burn brightly for eternity.

As they reveled in the bliss of their union, Lily and Adi knew that they were destined to be together to share their lives, their dreams, and their deepest desires. For in each other's arms, they had found the true meaning of love, a love that would endure the test of time and stand as a beacon of hope in a world consumed by darkness.

As time passed, cracks began to appear in Lily and Adi's once-perfect relationship. Small disagreements escalated into heated arguments, and soon, they found themselves immersed in a cycle of conflict and tension. Misunderstandings festered, communication faltered, and the distance between them grew wider with each passing day.

Their once-cherished bond now strained under the weight of unresolved issues and unspoken grievances. Words left unspoken hung heavy in the air, casting a shadow over their once-bright love.

Despite their best efforts to salvage their relationship, Lily and Adi found themselves drifting further apart, their hearts heavy with the burden of unspoken words and unresolved conflicts.

Amidst the turmoil, Lily found solace in the unwavering support of her friends, who stood by her side through thick and thin. They lent her a listening ear, offering comfort and guidance as she navigated the rocky terrain of her relationship.

Desperate to mend the rift between Lily and Adi, Lily's friends intervened, attempting to bridge the gap and facilitate communication between the estranged lovers. They urged Adi to reconsider his stance, emphasizing the depth of Lily's love and the pain caused by their rift.

Despite their efforts, reconciliation remained elusive, and the silence between Lily and Adi stretched on, punctuated only by the echoes of their unresolved conflicts.

Yet amidst the darkness, a glimmer of hope remained a belief that love could conquer all obstacles and heal even the deepest wounds. With patience, understanding, and unwavering determination, Lily and Adi remained hopeful that they could find their way back to each other, stronger and more resilient than before.

ᑎᑎᑎ

Dreams fades

Myra and Adi were childhood friends who shared many memories growing up. They studied together until the 9th standard, enjoying each other's company and making the most of their school days. However, life took a turn when Myra's family had to relocate to another city due to her father's job transfer. After that, they lost touch, their friendship fading into distant memories. It seemed like their connection was just a passing phase of adolescence, soon forgotten as they moved on with their lives. Yet, fate had other plans. After almost five years of being apart, Myra and Adi unexpectedly crossed paths again, reigniting old memories and sparking new conversations.

As Adi's bond with Myra grew stronger, Lily found herself grappling with a storm of emotions that threatened to consume her. Each new photo, each shared moment captured on social media served as a painful reminder of the distance that had grown between her and Adi.

As Adi's attention turned towards Myra, Lily found herself fading into the background of his life. The love they once shared began to wither like a flower deprived of sunlight, replaced by the budding affection he felt for another. With each passing day, Adi's indifference towards Lily grew, leaving her bewildered and hurt. She watched helplessly as he blamed her for his own wandering heart, unable to comprehend how quickly his promises of eternal love had dissolved into thin air.

For Lily, the pain of Adi's betrayal cut deep, like a dagger to her heart. She questioned everything she thought she knew about their relationship, grappling with feelings of inadequacy and abandonment. The once bright future they had envisioned together now seemed shrouded in uncertainty, overshadowed by Adi's newfound infatuation with Myra.

Despite her anguish, Lily couldn't help but wonder what had changed in Adi's heart to make him turn away from her so abruptly. She searched for answers in the memories they had shared, desperately clinging to the hope that their love could be salvaged. But with each passing day, it became clear that Adi's affections now lay elsewhere, leaving Lily to confront the harsh reality that their love had faded away.

Unable to contain her sorrow, Lily's tears flowed freely, a silent testament to the ache that gripped her heart. She couldn't bear the thought of sharing Adi's affections with another, the very idea striking a deep and painful chord within her soul.

In the quiet solitude of her room, Lily allowed herself to succumb to the weight of her grief, her sobs echoing in the stillness of the night. She felt as though her world was crumbling around her, the love she had once cherished slipping through her fingers like grains of sand.

With each passing day, the pain of betrayal gnawed at Lily's spirit, leaving her feeling hollow and empty inside. She longed for the warmth of Adi's embrace, for the reassurance that their love was still strong and true. But with each new photo that appeared on her social media feed, her hopes were dashed anew, leaving her feeling more lost and alone than ever before.

Despite her best efforts to hold onto hope, Lily couldn't shake the feeling of despair that clung to her like a shadow. She knew that she couldn't continue to live in denial, to pretend that everything was fine when her heart was breaking into a million pieces.

And so, with tears streaming down her cheeks, Lily made a difficult decision to confront Adi and lay bare the depths of her pain. She couldn't allow herself to suffer in silence any longer, to watch idly as the love she had once held so dear slipped away from her grasp.

Summoning every ounce of courage she possessed, Lily approached Adi, her voice trembling with emotion as she poured out her heart. She told him of the agony she had endured, of the tears she had shed in secret, and of the unbearable pain of seeing him with another.

But Adi's response was not what Lily had hoped for. Instead of understanding and compassion, she was met with defensiveness and indifference. Adi brushed off her concerns, dismissing her fears as unfounded and unwarranted.

In that moment, Lily realized that she had lost more than just a lover she had lost the person she thought she knew, the person she had trusted with her heart. And as she turned away, her heart heavy with sorrow, she knew that the road ahead would be long and difficult, but she also knew that she was strong enough to walk it alone.

Despite Lily's initial reluctance to leave the confines of her room, her friends refused to stand idly by while she suffered in silence. Concerned for her well-being, they gently urged her to join them for a much-needed outing, hoping to lift her spirits and offer her a brief respite from her pain.

Though Lily initially resisted their efforts, her friends' persistence eventually paid off, and she reluctantly agreed to accompany them to the shopping mall. As they strolled through the bustling corridors, Lily's thoughts were consumed by the weight of her sorrow, her eyes downcast and her steps heavy with despair.

But amidst the sea of faces, Lily's gaze fell upon a familiar figure a figure that sent a jolt of shock coursing through her veins. There, standing before her, was Myra the very person who had unwittingly become the source of her anguish.

For a moment, time seemed to stand still as Lily and Myra locked eyes, the air thick with tension and unspoken emotions. In that fleeting moment, Lily felt a surge of conflicting emotions wash over her anger, betrayal, and a profound sense of sadness.

But as she looked into Myra's eyes, Lily saw something unexpected a flicker of empathy and understanding that softened the edges of her pain. In that moment, she realized that Myra was not the enemy she had perceived her to be, but rather, a fellow traveler on the tumultuous journey of love.

As Lily gazed into Myra's eyes, a torrent of questions flooded her mind, each one a plea for answers to the turmoil that had consumed her heart. With bated breath, she waited for Myra's response, her heart pounding in her chest as she braced herself for the truth.

In a voice tinged with sadness, Myra began to speak, her words carrying the weight of shared memories and lost love. She spoke of Adi a boy who had once been her closest confidant, her childhood companion, and her first love. They had shared a bond forged in the innocence of youth, their hearts entwined in the sweet promise of forever.

But as the years passed and life took them down different paths, their love began to wane, fading like the dying embers of a once-bright flame. They drifted apart, their connection severed by the cruel hand of fate and the relentless march of time.

With a heavy heart, Myra recounted how she had left for another city to pursue her studies, leaving behind the echoes of their shared past. For a time, they had lost touch, their memories fading into the recesses of their minds like forgotten dreams.

But fate had other plans, for it was on the vast expanse of social media that Adi and Myra's paths crossed once more, their hearts drawn together by the invisible threads of fate. They began to talk and chat, their conversations a balm to the wounds of time and distance.

And so, against all odds, they found themselves falling in love once again, their hearts reclaiming the connection that had once been lost. For six months, they had been together, their love blossoming anew in the fertile soil of their shared history.

With a heavy heart, Myra revealed the painful truth that Adi had told her that he and Lily had already parted ways, their love shattered by the harsh realities of life and love. And as she spoke, Lily felt the weight of her words settle like a stone in the pit of her stomach, a bitter reminder of the love that had slipped through her fingers like grains of sand.

As Lily stood there, her heart heavy with sorrow and her mind reeling from the revelations that Myra had shared, she found herself unable to utter a single word. Her friends, sensing her distress, exchanged knowing glances before silently agreeing to leave the place.

As they bid farewell to Myra, Lily felt a pang of sadness wash over her a sadness born from the knowledge that the girl who had once been the source of her pain was also a victim of circumstance, a fellow traveler on the unpredictable journey of love.

Gently guiding Lily away from the tumultuous sea of emotions that threatened to engulf her, her friends led her back to the sanctuary of her hostel room. With tender care, they offered her words of comfort and solace, their presence a balm to her wounded spirit.

Once they were alone, Lily's tears flowed freely, her sobs echoing in the stillness of the room. With trembling hands, she reached for her phone, her heart heavy with dread as she dialed Adi's number.

As Adi's voice filled the line, Lily's heart clenched with fear, knowing that the words she longed to hear would bring her nothing but pain. And when Adi spoke, his words were like a dagger to her heart cold and unforgiving.

He accused her of being insecure and possessive, of suffocating him with her need for reassurance and validation. And then, in a single, crushing blow, he declared that their relationship was over that he no longer loved her and had no desire to be with her.

As the weight of his words settled over her like a heavy blanket, Lily felt as though the world had come crashing down around her. She pleaded and begged, her voice raw with desperation, but Adi's resolve remained unyielding.

With a final, heart-wrenching farewell, Adi cut the call, leaving Lily alone with her shattered dreams and broken heart. In the silence that followed, Lily's cries filled the room, a mournful lament for the love she had lost and the future that would never be.

As the hours passed and the tears continued to fall, Lily felt as though she were drowning in a sea of despair.

As the weight of her heartache threatened to crush her spirit, Lily found herself consumed by a darkness so profound, it felt as though it would swallow her whole. The pain of Adi's rejection gnawed at her soul, leaving her feeling raw and exposed, her emotions laid bare for the world to see.

In the grip of her despair, Lily's thoughts turned to escape from the relentless ache that consumed her, the constant reminder of the love she had lost. With trembling hands and tears streaming down her cheeks, she reached for anything that would offer relief from the torment of her shattered dreams.

In her anguish, Lily turned to the only solace she could find the prospect of ending her pain once and for all. The thought of taking her own life seemed like the only way to escape the unbearable agony of living without Adi by her side.

With a heart heavy with sorrow and a mind clouded by despair, Lily resolved to end her suffering, to silence the voices of doubt and despair that echoed in her mind. She sought refuge in the darkness, seeking solace in the oblivion that awaited her on the other side.

Amidst the storm of Lily's inner turmoil, her friends stood as beacons of light in the darkness, unwavering in their commitment to stand by her side through every trial and tribulation. Sensing Lily's pain and the dangerous depths of her despair, they refused to leave her alone, knowing that her fragile state of mind left her vulnerable to the seductive whispers of self-destruction.

Through countless sleepless nights and tear-stained days, Lily's friends remained steadfast in their support, offering a shoulder to cry on and a listening ear to hear her cries of anguish. They held her close, shielding her from the full force of her pain, and reminding her that she was not alone that she was loved, cherished, and valued beyond measure.

As the seasons changed and the years slipped by, Lily's friends became her lifeline, guiding her through the tumultuous waters of her inner turmoil with unwavering compassion and empathy. Together, they weathered the storms of her despair, emerging stronger and more resilient with each passing day.

And now, as they entered their final year of college, Lily's friends remained by her side, their bond forged in the fires of adversity stronger than ever before. With their unwavering support and steadfast love, they helped to carry Lily through the darkest days, lighting the way towards a brighter tomorrow.

Though the road ahead was fraught with uncertainty and challenges yet to be faced, Lily knew that as long as she had her friends by her side, she could weather any storm, overcome any obstacle, and emerge victorious in the end. For in the embrace of their friendship, she found the strength to carry on, to face each new day with courage and resilience, and to never lose hope in the promise of a brighter tomorrow.

As Lily absentmindedly scrolled through her phone, her heart heavy with the weight of her sorrow, she stumbled upon a series of pictures that stopped her dead in her tracks. With a gasp of disbelief, the device slipped from her trembling fingers, clattering to the ground below.

Her eyes flooded with tears as she gazed at the images before her a collection of snaps that captured moments of joy and laughter, scenes of Adi and Myra together, their smiles radiant and their laughter infectious. Each image was like a dagger to her heart, piercing her soul with the cruel reminder of what she had lost.

"Its Adi and Myra wedding pictures"

Unable to bear the sight any longer, Lily buried her face in her hands, her body racked with sobs of anguish. The tears flowed freely, unchecked and unbidden, as the pain of betrayal washed over her like a tidal wave, threatening to engulf her in its relentless grip.

In that moment of despair, Lily felt as though her world was crumbling around her, the foundations of her reality shaken to their core. Every cherished memory, every whispered promise, now tainted by the specter of betrayal and deceit. With a trembling hand, Lily reached for her phone, her fingers tracing the contours of the screen with a sense of resignation. And as she stared at the images once more, a hollow ache settled in the pit of her stomach, a gnawing emptiness that seemed to consume her from within.

As Lily's eyes fixated on the images before her, her heart sank like a stone in the depths of despair. The phone slipped from her trembling hands, crashing to the ground with a resounding thud, as her mind struggled to comprehend the devastating truth laid bare before her.

The words echoed in Lily's mind like a mournful dirge, each syllable a cruel reminder of the betrayal that had torn her world asunder. Adi and Myra smiling, radiant, entwined in each other's arms, their happiness captured for eternity in the photographs that now mocked Lily's shattered dreams.

A strangled cry escaped Lily's lips as the weight of the betrayal crashed over her like a tidal wave, threatening to drown her in its suffocating embrace. How could this be happening? How could Adi, the love of her life, pledge his heart to another, leaving Lily cast aside like a discarded relic of the past?

Her chest constricted with a pain so visceral, it felt as though her very soul was being torn asunder. The tears flowed unabated now, a torrent of anguish and heartache that threatened to consume her whole. How could she have been so blind, so foolish to believe in a love that was nothing more than a cruel facade?

With trembling hands, Lily reached for her phone once more, her fingers tracing the outline of Adi's face in the photographs with a mixture of longing and loathing. The man she had loved, the man she had trusted with her heart, now stood before her as a stranger a betrayer, a deceiver, a phantom haunting the ruins of her shattered dreams.

And as the reality of Adi's betrayal sank in, Lily felt a searing rage ignite within her a firestorm of fury and indignation that threatened to consume her from within. How dare he? How dare he pledge his love to another, leaving Lily to pick up the shattered pieces of her heart?

But beneath the rage and the sorrow, beneath the crushing weight of her despair, a flicker of defiance burned bright within Lily's soul. Though broken and bruised, she refused to be defeated not by Adi, not by Myra, not by anyone.

With a steely resolve, Lily wiped away her tears, her jaw set in a firm line of determination. She may have been betrayed, she may have been cast aside, but she refused to let this be the end of her story. But even as she contemplated her own demise, a tiny voice whispered in the depths of her soul a voice that spoke of hope and resilience, of the possibility of healing and redemption. And in that moment of clarity, Lily realized that she was not alone that there were those who loved her, who would stand by her side through even the darkest of nights.

With a newfound determination coursing through her veins, Lily made a choice a choice to fight for her life, to cling to the flicker of hope that burned within her heart. Though the road ahead would be fraught with challenges and obstacles, she refused to surrender to despair, to let the darkness win. And so, with a steely resolve and a heart full of courage, Lily vowed to face each new day with strength and determination, to rise above the pain and sorrow that threatened to consume her. For she knew that even in her darkest hour, there was light to be found that within her lay the power to overcome even the greatest of trials.

She may have been betrayed, she may have been cast aside, but she refused to let this be the end of her story. For amidst the ruins of her shattered dreams, a glimmer of hope still remained a promise of redemption, of renewal, of a future yet unwritten. And with that promise burning bright in her heart, Lily gathered the shattered remnants of her pride and her dignity, and with a resolute step forward, she began to forge a new path one free from the shadows of betrayal, one guided by the light of her own unwavering strength.

As the days turned into weeks and the weeks into months, Lily found solace in the passage of time. With each sunrise and sunset, the wounds inflicted upon her heart began to heal, slowly but surely, as she embarked on the journey of moving on from her painful past.

With a newfound sense of resilience and determination, Lily set her sights on a brighter future, one filled with promise and possibility. And as fate would have it, an opportunity arose that would pave the way for her to leave behind the ghosts of her past and start afresh in a new city a city brimming with opportunity and adventure.

With a sense of trepidation and excitement coursing through her veins, Lily made the bold decision to pursue her master's degree in a different city, far removed from the memories that still haunted her in the place she once called home. It was a chance for her to reinvent herself, to carve out a new identity, free from the shadows of her past.

And so, with a heavy heart and a hopeful spirit, Lily bid farewell to the familiar streets and faces of her old life, and set out on a journey into the unknown. Armed with nothing but her dreams and determination, she ventured forth into the great unknown, ready to embrace whatever the future held for her.

ppp

5

New beginning: New City

Lily opted for Pune to pursue her master's degree. In the city of her new college, Lily found herself immersed in a world of endless possibilities. The campus, with its lush greenery and sprawling grounds, provided a refreshing escape from the hustle and bustle of city life. As she settled into her new surroundings, Lily discovered a sense of camaraderie among her peers, forging friendships.

Lily found herself gradually letting go of the pain and heartache that had once consumed her. She immersed herself in her studies, throwing herself wholeheartedly into the pursuit of knowledge and learning. And with each passing day, she felt a little lighter, a little freer, as the weight of her past began to lift from her shoulders.

In the hustle of her new life, Lily discovered a sense of purpose and fulfillment that she had never known before. She forged new friendships, explored new passions, and embraced new experiences with an open heart and an open mind. And as she looked back on the journey that had brought her to this moment, Lily realized that while the scars of her past would always remain, they no longer defined her. She was no longer the broken-hearted girl who had been betrayed by love she was stronger, wiser, and more resilient than she had ever been before.

Though the hostel food left much to be desired, Lily found solace in the company of her roommates, who quickly became like family to her. Together, they navigated the ups and downs of college life, sharing laughter and late-night study sessions in equal measure.

Amidst the chaos of college life, Lily found sanctuary in the classroom, where she was met with warmth and encouragement from her professors. With their guidance, she delved into her studies with renewed enthusiasm, eager to soak up knowledge like a sponge.

But it wasn't just academics that shaped Lily's college experience it was the moments of laughter shared with friends, the quiet moments of reflection beneath the shade of a sprawling tree, and the countless adventures embarked upon in pursuit of new experiences.

As the days turned into weeks and the weeks into months, Lily felt herself slowly but surely healing from the wounds of her past. The pain and heartache that had once consumed her began to fade into the background, replaced by a sense of hope and optimism for the future.

As the final days of Lily's master's program approached, she found herself reflecting on the journey that had brought her to this moment. Over the course of two years, she had experienced a whirlwind of emotions, faced numerous challenges, and emerged stronger and more confident than ever before.

Throughout her time in college, Lily had embraced every opportunity that came her way, whether it was participating in academic competitions, leading student organizations, or engaging in community service projects. And with each new experience, she had gained valuable insights into herself and the world around her.

Despite the occasional ups and downs that came with navigating the rigors of academia, Lily had persevered, fueled by her unwavering determination to succeed. And as the end of her master's program drew near, she found herself standing at the top of her class, basking in the glow of her academic achievements.

It was a proud moment for Lily when she was acknowledged as the topper of her college, her hard work and dedication finally paying off in the form of recognition and praise from her peers and professors alike. She reveled in the sense of accomplishment that came with knowing that she had surpassed even her own expectations.

But beyond the accolades and honors, what truly made Lily's college experience memorable were the friendships she had forged along the way. From her roommates in the hostel to her classmates and juniors, each person she met had left an indelible mark on her heart.

As the time for farewell approached, Lily found herself filled with a mix of emotions. On one hand, she was excited to embark on the next chapter of her life, armed with the knowledge and skills she had acquired during her time in college. On the other hand, she couldn't help but feel a pang of sadness at the thought of leaving behind the friends and memories she had made along the way.

The farewell ceremony was a poignant affair, filled with laughter, tears, and heartfelt speeches. As each person took turns sharing their favorite memories and expressing their gratitude for the time they had spent together, Lily couldn't help but feel a sense of gratitude for the bonds of friendship that had sustained her throughout her college journey.

And as the final farewells were exchanged and hugs were shared, Lily knew that while her time in college may have come to an end, the friendships she had formed would last a lifetime. With a smile on her face and a heart full of memories, she stepped out into the world and ready to embrace future.

❥❥❥

New Phase of life: Career & Job

As Lily completed her master's degree, she felt a surge of excitement and anticipation for the next chapter of her life. The prospect of finally achieving independence and making her mark in the professional world filled her with a sense of purpose and determination. With her education serving as a solid foundation, Lily eagerly began her job search, eager to find a position that would align with her skills, values, and aspirations.

Applying for various job opportunities, Lily soon found herself inundated with interview requests and job offers. Each offer brought with it a unique set of possibilities and challenges, leaving Lily with the daunting task of deciding which path to pursue. She knew that this decision would shape not only her immediate future but also her long-term career trajectory, and she approached it with a mixture of excitement and apprehension.

Taking a methodical approach, Lily carefully evaluated each job offer, considering factors such as job responsibilities, company culture, growth potential, and alignment with her personal and professional goals. She sought advice from mentors, consulted with friends and family, and conducted thorough research to ensure she made an informed decision.

Amidst the flurry of offers, one opportunity stood out to Lily: the position of educational coordinator at Hope Academy. This role spoke to her passion for education and her desire to make a positive impact on the lives of young people. The mission of Hope Academy, with its focus on empowering students and fostering academic excellence, resonated deeply with Lily, and she saw it as an opportunity to contribute to a cause she believed in wholeheartedly.

After much deliberation and soul-searching, Lily made the decision to accept the job offer from Hope Academy. It was a choice driven not only by her career aspirations but also by her values and sense of purpose. She felt a sense of excitement and anticipation as she prepared to embark on this new chapter of her life, eager to bring her skills, passion, and dedication to her role as an educational coordinator.

Lily's first day at the office was a mix of nerves and excitement. As she entered the building, located in the bustling center of the city, she couldn't help but feel a sense of anticipation for the journey that lay ahead. With each step she took, her heart beat a little faster, and she couldn't wait to dive into her new role.

Upon arrival, Lily was warmly greeted by her manager, Mrs. Laila. With a friendly smile, Mrs. Laila welcomed Lily to the team and introduced her to the other colleagues in the office. Lily felt a wave of relief wash over her as she was met with friendly faces and warm greetings. She knew that she was in good hands.

Mrs. Laila then took Lily on a tour of the office, showing her around the various departments and introducing her to the layout of the workspace. As they walked, Mrs. Laila explained Lily's responsibilities and what was expected of her in her new role as an educational coordinator.

Lily listened intently, absorbing every detail as Mrs. Laila outlined the scope of her work. She felt a sense of purpose and determination building within her, eager to make a positive impact in her new position. Mrs. Laila's guidance and support reassured Lily that she was in the right place, surrounded by a team that believed in her abilities.

After the tour, Mrs. Laila took Lily to her workstation, where she would be spending much of her time. Lily felt a surge of excitement as she settled into her new surroundings, eager to dive into her tasks and contribute to the mission of Hope Academy.

Throughout the day, Lily familiarized herself with her duties, diving into her work with enthusiasm and determination. She spent time getting to know her colleagues, asking questions, and seeking guidance whenever she needed it. Despite the inevitable nerves that come with starting a new job, Lily felt a sense of belonging and camaraderie within the office.

As the day drew to a close, Lily reflected on her first day with a sense of satisfaction and pride. She had navigated the challenges of starting a new job with grace and confidence, and she was excited to see what the future held.

As Lily settled into her new role at Hope Academy, she found herself immersed in the daily routines of office life. Her workstation, located opposite a boy from another team, intrigued her from the moment she arrived. Despite their proximity, they had yet to exchange words, as he had been on leave for the first two days of her tenure.

The boy's absence had left Lily curious about him. She couldn't help but steal glances in his direction, wondering about the person behind the face that sat across from her. Their workstations were divided by a small wooden cabin, yet they were positioned in such a way that they faced each other directly, allowing for occasional glimpses into each other's worlds.

As Lily focused on her tasks, she couldn't shake the feeling of intrigue that surrounded the mysterious boy. She found herself stealing glances in his direction whenever she could, trying to catch a glimpse of his features and discern more about him. Despite her curiosity, she hesitated to initiate conversation, unsure of how to break the silence that lingered between them.

Similarly, the boy seemed engrossed in his work, his attention fixed on his computer screen as he diligently tackled his tasks. Though they were mere feet apart, they remained worlds apart, each absorbed in their own responsibilities and thoughts.

Days passed, and still, the silence between Lily and the boy persisted. Despite their proximity, they remained strangers, their interactions limited to fleeting glances and polite nods. Yet, there was an unspoken connection between them, a sense of familiarity that belied their lack of formal introduction.

As time went on, Lily couldn't shake the feeling that there was more to the boy than met the eye. She found herself growing increasingly curious about him, yearning to unravel the mystery that shrouded his presence in the office. Yet, she hesitated to approach him, unsure of how he would respond to her sudden intrusion into his world.

Meanwhile, the boy couldn't help but notice Lily's curious glances in his direction. Though he remained focused on his work, her presence lingered in the back of his mind, a constant source of intrigue and fascination. He found himself wondering about the girl who sat opposite him, her quiet demeanor and thoughtful expressions capturing his attention.

৩৩৩

Inception of Love

In the soft morning light, before the office began, Lily found herself drawn to mysterious boy's desk. It had been nearly three weeks since she had first laid eyes on him, and yet, she still didn't know his name. Determined to uncover this mystery, she approached his workstation with a sense of anticipation, her heart fluttering with excitement.

As she reached his desk, Lily couldn't help but feel a sense of nervousness wash over her. What if someone saw her snooping around? What if the mysterious boy caught her in the act? Pushing aside her doubts, she took a deep breath and leaned in closer, her eyes scanning the various papers and documents scattered across his desk.

Amidst the clutter, Lily's gaze fell upon a small, inconspicuous object – a nameplate tucked away in a corner. It seemed almost as if it were hidden on purpose, waiting to be discovered. With bated breath, Lily reached out and picked it up, her heart pounding in her chest.

As she turned the nameplate over, her eyes widened in surprise. There, in elegant script, was a name she had longed to know. Its "Surya". Lily felt a surge of triumph wash over her as she absorbed the beauty of his name. It was like uncovering a long-lost secret, a piece of the puzzle that had been missing for so long.

With a satisfied smile, Lily stepped back from the desk, her mission accomplished. She had finally learned his name, and it felt like a small victory in the grand scheme of things. As she made her way back to her own workstation, she couldn't shake the feeling of pride that swelled within her.

Throughout the day, as she immersed herself in her work, Lily found herself stealing glances at Surya from time to time. Now that she knew his name, he seemed more real, more tangible somehow. She found herself wondering about him: his interests, his hobbies, his dreams.

Despite their newfound connection, Lily remained hesitant to approach Surya directly. She didn't want to come across as too eager or intrusive, and so she contented herself with admiring him from afar, savoring the small moments they shared in passing.

As the day wore on, Lily couldn't help but feel a sense of warmth and contentment settle over her. She had taken a leap of faith, and it had paid off in ways she hadn't expected. Knowing Surya's name felt like the beginning of something new, a spark of connection that had the potential to ignite into something more.

And so, with a heart full of hope and anticipation, Lily allowed herself to dream of what the future might hold a future where she and Surya could share more than just fleeting glances and stolen moments, but a bond that was deep and meaningful, forged in the quiet moments of a bustling office.

As the days turned into weeks and the weeks into months, Lily and Surya found themselves caught in a silent dance of longing and curiosity. Despite sitting opposite each other day after day, they had never exchanged more than fleeting glances and polite nods.

Two months had passed since Lily had discovered Surya's name, yet their interactions remained limited to silent observations from across the room. It was as if an invisible barrier separated them, keeping their worlds from colliding despite their physical proximity.

For Lily, each day brought with it a mixture of hope and frustration. She longed to break through the walls of silence that surrounded Surya, to bridge the gap between them and discover the person behind the name. Yet, fear and uncertainty held her back, whispering doubts in her ear and keeping her rooted in place.

Similarly, Surya seemed to keep his distance, his attention focused solely on his work as he navigated the complexities of office life. Though Lily caught glimpses of him throughout the day a fleeting smile here, a furrowed brow there he remained an enigma, his thoughts and feelings hidden from view.

Despite their lack of communication, the air between them crackled with unspoken tension, a palpable energy that seemed to linger long after they had gone their separate ways. It was as if the mere presence of the other was enough to stir something deep within them, igniting a spark that refused to be extinguished.

And so, as the days stretched on and the seasons changed, Lily and Surya continued their silent dance, each step bringing them closer to the edge of something unknown. Whether they would ever find the courage to take that final leap remained to be seen, but one thing was certain their connection, though silent, was undeniable, weaving its way through the fabric of their everyday lives and binding them together in ways they could never have imagined.

As Lily immersed herself in the melodies of her favorite songs, there was one in particular that seemed to speak directly to her soul. With each lyric and every note, it felt as though the song had been written especially for her and Surya.

"I like your eyes, you look away when you pretend not to care" I like the dimples on the corners of the smile that you wear".

These words resonated deeply with Lily, echoing her own thoughts and feelings about the man seated across from her. She found herself playing the song on repeat, losing herself in its haunting melody and poignant lyrics.

With each listen, Lily felt a sense of connection and understanding wash over her, as though the songwriter had somehow tapped into the essence of her relationship with Surya. It was as if the music had become a conduit for their unspoken emotions, a silent witness to the silent dance they shared.

And so, as the song filled the air around her, Lily couldn't help but feel a flicker of hope ignite within her heart. Perhaps, just perhaps, the music held the key to unlocking the barriers between her and Surya, allowing them to finally break free from the confines of their silent world and embrace the love that lay waiting just beyond their reach.

Despite the budding connection between Lily and Surya, Lily carried with her the scars of her past. The pain and trauma she had endured made it difficult for her to trust again, to open herself up to the possibility of love. So, instead of dwelling on what could be, Lily found solace in simply enjoying the presence of Surya.

For six long months, they continued their silent dance, their unspoken words hanging in the air between them like a delicate thread. Lily couldn't deny the growing attraction she felt towards Surya, nor could she ignore the longing in his eyes whenever their gazes met.

Yet, as much as she yearned to break free from the shackles of her past, fear held her back. Fear of getting hurt again, fear of repeating the mistakes of the past, fear of allowing herself to be vulnerable once more. And so, she remained content to bask in the warmth of Surya's presence, without daring to take that final leap of faith.

Each day brought with it a fresh wave of emotions, a tug-of-war between the desire to move forward and the fear of what lay ahead. Lily found herself caught in a constant battle with her own insecurities, her heart torn between the longing for connection and the need to protect herself from further pain.

But despite the darkness that lingered within her, there was a glimmer of hope, a tiny spark of possibility that refused to be extinguished.

Deep down, Lily knew that Surya held the key to unlocking the chains that bound her heart. Despite his gentle demeanor, Surya was a dedicated workaholic, his focus firmly fixed on his professional responsibilities. Lily couldn't help but admire his commitment to his work, his unwavering dedication evident in the way he approached each task with precision and diligence.

Day after day, Lily watched from a far as Surya immersed himself in his work, his attention never wavering, his determination unwavering. He seemed oblivious to the world around him, lost in the intricate web of numbers and data that filled his computer screen.

As the months passed, Lily's curiosity about Surya only grew stronger, her fascination with this enigmatic man deepening with each passing day. Yet, despite her best efforts to strike up a conversation, their interactions remained limited to fleeting glances and silent nods of acknowledgment.

It seemed as though they were trapped in a silent dance, their words left unspoken, their feelings hidden beneath a veil of secrecy. And while Lily longed to break through the walls that separated them, to bridge the gap between them with words of friendship and understanding, she couldn't help but feel intimidated by Surya's stoic demeanor.

Nevertheless, she remained determined to uncover the mystery that surrounded him, to unravel the layers of complexity that shrouded his true nature. For beneath his outwardly composed facade, Lily sensed a kindred spirit, a soul yearning for connection and understanding.

And so, she continued to observe him from a far, her silent vigil a testament to the silent bond that had formed between them. Though they may not have exchanged words, their silent companionship spoke volumes, each fleeting glance and shared moment a silent affirmation of the connection that bound them together.

Lily found herself drawn ever closer to Surya, her heart inexplicably drawn to his quiet strength and unwavering determination. And though their journey had been fraught with silence and uncertainty, Lily remained hopeful that one day, they would find the courage to break free from the chains that bound them and embrace the love that awaited them on the other side.

As the urgency of Mrs. Laila's request weighed heavily on Lily's mind, she knew that the time had come to finally break the silence that had lingered between her and Surya for far too long. With a heart pounding with nervous anticipation, Lily made her way to Surya's desk, her steps faltering slightly as she approached him.

"Um, hi Surya," Lily began tentatively, her voice barely above a whisper as she struggled to find the right words to say. "I... I need some data for Mrs. Laila. It's urgent."

Surya looked up from his computer screen, his expression unreadable as he regarded Lily with a calm detachment. "Sure, Lily. What do you need?" he replied, his tone polite but reserved.

Lily felt a surge of relief wash over her as Surya offered his assistance, his willingness to help easing some of the tension that had been building inside her. Taking a deep breath to steady her nerves, Lily explained the specifics of the data she required, her words coming out in a rush as she tried to articulate herself clearly.

Surya listened attentively, nodding in understanding as Lily outlined her request. With a few deft clicks of his mouse, he pulled up the necessary information on his computer screen, his fingers moving swiftly over the keyboard as he navigated through the database.

"Here you go, Lily," Surya said, turning his monitor towards her so she could see the data for herself. "I've compiled everything you need into a spreadsheet. Let me know if there's anything else I can help you with."

Lily's eyes widened in surprise as she glanced at the screen, impressed by the thoroughness of Surya's work. "Th-thank you, Surya," she stammered, her cheeks flushing with embarrassment as she realized just how flustered she must appear.

Surya offered her a small smile, his eyes crinkling at the corners as he returned to his own work. "No problem, Lily. Glad I could help," he replied, his tone warm and genuine.

As Lily returned to her desk, a sense of accomplishment washed over her, mingled with a newfound sense of admiration for Surya. Though their conversation had been brief, it had opened the door to a new level of understanding between them, one that held the promise of a deeper connection yet to come.

And as she sifted through the data on her computer screen, Lily couldn't help but feel a sense of gratitude for the unexpected bond that had begun to form between her and Surya, a bond that had blossomed from the seeds of a simple request and the willingness to reach out and break the silence that had kept them apart for so long.

As the next day she required more data from Surya. She reached his desk to collect the data from him.

As Lily stood beside Surya's desk, her attention focused on the data he was presenting to her, she couldn't shake the feeling of nervous anticipation that tingled through her veins. Surya's explanations were clear and concise, his fingers moving deftly over the keyboard as he navigated through the spreadsheet on his computer screen.

But as he pointed out a particular section of the data, his hand inadvertently brushed against Lily's, sending a jolt of electricity coursing through her body. Time seemed to stand still in that fleeting moment, the tension between them palpable as their eyes met, both of them frozen in place by the unexpected intimacy of the gesture.

For Lily, it was as if the world had narrowed down to the sensation of Surya's touch, the warmth of his hand searing into her skin and igniting a firestorm of emotions within her. Her heart raced in her chest, her breath catching in her throat as she struggled to process the flood of sensations that threatened to overwhelm her.

Surya, too, seemed momentarily stunned by the contact, his gaze locking with Lily's in a silent exchange of shared awareness. In that brief instant, something shifted between them, a silent acknowledgment of the unspoken connection that had been simmering beneath the surface all along. But as quickly as it had begun, the moment passed, and Surya withdrew his hand, the spell broken by the mundane reality of their surroundings. Clearing his throat awkwardly, he resumed his explanation, though the air between them crackled with a newfound tension that neither could ignore.

For Lily, the memory of that fleeting touch lingered long after Surya had returned to his work, a tantalizing glimpse of the deeper connection that lay waiting to be explored.

And as she made her way back to her own desk, her mind whirled with the possibilities of what the future might hold, filled with the promise of a bond that transcended the confines of their professional relationship.

The next day dawned with a sense of anticipation tingling in the air, the memory of yesterday's fleeting touch lingering in Lily's mind like a half-forgotten dream. As she made her way to the office, her heart fluttered with nervous excitement, wondering if today would bring another opportunity for her and Surya to connect.

Sure enough, as the morning progressed, Mrs. Laila approached Lily with another task that required her to seek assistance from Surya. This time, it was a problem with her spreadsheet that needed Surya's expertise to resolve. Lily felt a mixture of trepidation and anticipation as she approached his desk once more, her pulse quickening with each step.

As she reached his workstation, she found Surya engrossed in his work, his brow furrowed in concentration as he studied the screen before him. Summoning her courage, Lily cleared her throat softly to announce her presence, causing Surya to look up in surprise.

Their eyes met, and for a moment, time seemed to stand still as they shared a silent exchange, the unspoken tension between them crackling in the air. But before either of them could speak, Lily quickly launched into an explanation of the issue she was facing with her spreadsheet, hoping to distract herself from the overwhelming rush of emotions threatening to engulf her.

Surya listened attentively, his gaze never leaving Lily's face as she spoke. His presence felt both reassuring and disconcerting at the same time, his proximity stirring up a whirlwind of conflicting emotions within her.

As Lily finished explaining the problem, she fell silent, her eyes locking with Surya's in a silent plea for assistance. For a moment, neither of them spokes, the weight of unspoken words hanging heavy in the air between them.

Then, without a word, Surya gestured for Lily to take a seat beside him, offering to help her troubleshoot the issue together. Lily hesitated for a moment, her heart pounding in her chest, before nodding gratefully and sinking into the chair beside him.

For the next few minutes, they worked in companionable silence, their shoulders brushing against each other as they hunched over the computer screen. Despite the tension that still simmered beneath the surface, there was a sense of ease in their interactions, a shared understanding that transcended the need for words.

And as they finally resolved the issue with the spreadsheet, Lily felt a sense of relief wash over her, mingled with a newfound sense of closeness to Surya. Though their relationship was still shrouded in uncertainty, she couldn't deny the spark of connection that had ignited between them, a flicker of hope in the darkness of the unknown.

As the days passed by, Lily and Surya found themselves crossing paths more frequently, often encountering each other in the confines of the office elevator. Despite being alone together in the confined space, an unspoken agreement seemed to settle between them, enveloping them in a cloak of silence.

Each time they stepped into the elevator, the air grew heavy with anticipation, the silence between them echoing like a cavernous void. Though their eyes would meet in brief glances, neither dared to break the quiet with idle chatter, contenting themselves with polite nods and murmured greetings.

As the elevator ascended or descended, the only sound that filled the space was the soft hum of the machinery, punctuated by the occasional ding as they reached their desired floor. In those fleeting moments, time seemed to stand still, the outside world fading away as they stood in silent communion, each lost in their own thoughts.

One fine morning, Lily and Surya found themselves arriving at the office earlier than usual, greeted only by the soft hum of the air conditioning and the gentle glow of the morning sun filtering through the windows. With just a few others from different teams scattered about, the office felt unusually quiet and serene.

Taking advantage of the quietude, Lily mustered the courage to break the silence, offering a tentative "hello" to Surya as she settled into her desk. Surprised by the unexpected greeting, Surya returned the gesture with a polite smile, his eyes crinkling at the corners in genuine warmth.

Encouraged by his response, Lily found herself emboldened to strike up a conversation, her curiosity piqued by the mystery of the man sitting opposite her. "So, where are you from?" she asked, her voice filled with genuine interest.

Surya's lips quirked into a small smile as he leaned back in his chair, contemplating her question for a moment before replying, "I'm from Indore, Madhya Pradesh, originally. What about you?"

Lily's eyes widened in surprise at his response. "I'm from Hyderabad," she answered, a hint of nostalgia tingeing her voice as she reminisced about her hometown. "It's quite a change being here in Pune, isn't it?"

Their conversation flowed effortlessly from there, weaving through topics ranging from their respective hometowns to their favorite foods and hobbies. As they exchanged stories and shared anecdotes, a sense of familiarity began to blossom between them, bridging the gap that had once seemed insurmountable.

Despite the early hour, time seemed to slip away unnoticed as they talked, lost in the simple pleasure of each other's company. For Lily, the encounter felt like a breath of fresh air, a welcome respite from the monotony of her daily routine. And for Surya, it was a rare opportunity to connect with someone on a deeper level, to let down the walls he had built around himself and allow someone new into his world.

As the morning sun climbed higher in the sky and the rest of the office began to stir to life, Lily and Surya reluctantly bid each other farewell, their brief encounter leaving a lingering warmth in its wake. And though they returned to their respective tasks with a newfound sense of purpose, they carried with them the memory of that serendipitous moment, a glimmer of hope amidst the chaos of the world around them.

As Lily settled into the comfort of her PG room after a long day at the office, her mind still lingered on the unexpected connection she had shared with Surya earlier that morning. Unable to shake off the lingering curiosity, she found herself instinctively reaching for her phone, her fingers tapping away in search of his elusive presence on social media.

With bated breath, she scrolled through profile after profile, hoping to stumble upon even a trace of him amidst the vast digital landscape. Yet, despite her best efforts, her searches yielded no results, leaving her feeling disheartened and disappointed.

It was as if Surya had vanished into thin air, leaving behind nothing but a fleeting memory of their brief encounter. Frustration gnawed at Lily's insides as she pondered the possibility of reconnecting with him, her mind swirling with unanswered questions and unspoken thoughts.

But amidst the disappointment, a spark of determination flickered to life within her. If she couldn't find Surya online, perhaps there was another way to track him down. With renewed resolve, Lily made a mental note to keep her eyes peeled for any opportunity to cross paths with him again, determined to unravel the mystery that surrounded the enigmatic man who had captured her curiosity and stolen her heart in the span of a single conversation.

The soft morning light filtered through the windows of the empty office, casting a warm glow upon Lily as she arrived early for another day of work. To her surprise, she spotted Surya already settled at his desk, his focused gaze fixed on his computer screen. A smile tugged at her lips as she greeted him with a cheerful "Good morning."

Surya returned her greeting with a nod, his expression brightening at the sight of her. With no one else around to disturb the quietude of the office, they found themselves drawn to each other, their conversation flowing effortlessly as they exchanged pleasantries.

As they chatted, Lily's curiosity piqued once more, and she mustered the courage to broach the topic of social media. "Do you happen to have an Instagram account?" she inquired, her voice laced with anticipation.

Surya nodded in affirmation, a hint of amusement dancing in his eyes. "Yes, I do," he replied, his tone tinged with a touch of intrigue. "Would you like to connect?"

Lily's heart leaped with joy at his response, and she nodded eagerly. "I'd love to," she exclaimed, her excitement palpable. With a few swift taps on their respective phones, they exchanged usernames and hit the 'Follow' button, forging a digital connection that mirrored the budding friendship blossoming between them.

As they settled back into their work routines, a newfound sense of camaraderie lingered in the air, each stolen glance and shared smile serving as a silent testament to the bond that was slowly forming between them.

Throughout the day, Lily found herself stealing glances at Surya, her heart fluttering with each fleeting moment of eye contact. The anticipation of exploring his Instagram profile filled her with a sense of anticipation, eager to delve deeper into the layers of his digital persona.

As the hours passed, Lily couldn't shake off the feeling of warmth that enveloped her whenever she was in Surya's presence. Despite the silence that permeated the office, their shared connection spoke volumes, bridging the gap between them and weaving an invisible thread of companionship that bound them together.

By the time the workday drew to a close, Lily found herself reluctant to part ways with Surya, a sense of longing tugging at her heartstrings. Yet, as they bid each other farewell with promises of meeting again the next day, she couldn't help but feel a newfound sense of hope blossoming within her.

As she made her way home, Lily's mind buzzed with thoughts of Surya, his Instagram profile beckoning to her like a treasure trove waiting to be discovered. With a sense of excitement bubbling in her chest, she eagerly anticipated the opportunity to delve into his digital world. She found immense joy as she gazed upon his pictures on Instagram, each image a testament to her happiness. With every picture, she found herself drawn deeper, her heart soaring with each glance at his profile. She found solace in immersing herself in his world, visiting his profile countless times. Each picture was like a window into her happiness and with every zoom, she felt her affection for him grow stronger, filling her with a sense of warmth and longing.

First Words of Digital Connection

The soft glow of her phone illuminated the darkness of Lily's room as she lay nestled beneath the covers, the gentle hum of the city outside lulling her into a state of calm. As the clock struck 11:30 p.m., a notification lit up her screen, drawing her attention to the message that had just arrived in her Instagram inbox.

With a flutter of excitement, Lily unlocked her phone to find a simple yet heartfelt message waiting for her: *"GOOD NIGHT LILY JI"* A warm smile tugged at the corners of her lips as she read the words, her heart swelling with happiness at the unexpected gesture of kindness.

But despite the joy that blossomed within her, Lily hesitated to respond. She lay in bed, her thoughts swirling with a mixture of emotions, unsure of how to react to Surya's message. A part of her longed to reciprocate the sentiment, to express her gratitude for his thoughtful gesture. Yet, another part of her feared the vulnerability that came with opening up to someone new.

In the end, Lily made a conscious decision to simply bask in the warmth of Surya's message, allowing its sweetness to wash over her like a comforting embrace. With a contented sigh, she set her phone aside and allowed herself to drift off into a peaceful slumber, the echoes of

Surya's words echoing in her mind as she slept soundly through the night.

The early morning light filtered through the windows of the office, casting a soft glow across the room as Lily and Surya settled into their respective workstations. As they began their tasks for the day, Surya couldn't help but feel a pang of curiosity about Lily's response or lack thereof to his message from the previous night.

With a gentle smile, he turned to Lily and asked, "Hey, why didn't you reply to my Instagram message last night?"

Caught off guard by his question, Lily paused for a moment before offering a sheepish smile in return. "Oh, I'm sorry. I actually went to bed pretty early last night, around 10 p.m. I must have missed your message."

Surya nodded understandingly. "No worries. It happens. We all need our rest, especially with the busy days we have ahead of us."

Relieved by his easygoing response, Lily returned her attention to her work, the lingering warmth of their conversation adding a touch of comfort to the tasks at hand. Despite the slight awkwardness of the moment, she found herself grateful for Surya's understanding and the effortless camaraderie that seemed to be blossoming between them.

Together, they delved into their work, their shared dedication to their tasks serving as a silent bond that transcended any fleeting moments of uncertainty. And as the day unfolded, Lily couldn't shake the feeling that perhaps, just perhaps, there was something special beginning to blossom between her and Surya a connection that went beyond the confines of their office walls.

As the days passed by, Lily and Surya's silent exchanges of glances became a regular occurrence in the office, each fleeting moment carrying with it a sense of unspoken connection between them. However, one day, Lily arrived at the office to find Surya's workstation empty, his absence casting a shadow over the familiar surroundings.

Alone in the office, Lily couldn't shake the feeling of longing that washed over her. She found herself missing Surya's presence more than she had anticipated, yearning for even just a glimpse of him to brighten her day. Determined to ease her solitude, Lily turned to Surya's Instagram profile, scrolling through his pictures with a mix of curiosity and fondness.

As she lingered over each image, she couldn't help but feel a sense of warmth wash over her a feeling of connection that transcended the boundaries of their office interactions. Lost in her thoughts, Lily found herself replaying their shared moments in her mind, each memory serving as a reminder of the budding friendship between them.

Then, on the day of Diwali, a message notification popped up on Lily's phone, momentarily stealing her attention from her work. With bated breath, she opened the message to find a heartfelt greeting from Surya: "Happy Diwali, Lily."

A smile spread across Lily's face as she read his words, her heart swelling with gratitude for his thoughtful gesture. In that moment, the loneliness that had weighed on her disappeared, replaced by a sense of warmth and connection that filled her with joy.

Quickly composing herself, Lily typed out a reply, expressing her thanks and returning the Diwali wishes to Surya. With each word, she poured her heart into the message, grateful for the opportunity to connect with him, even from afar.

As she hit send, a sense of contentment washed over her, filling her with a renewed sense of hope and optimism. In that simple exchange of messages, Lily found solace in the knowledge that no matter the distance between them, their bond would continue to thrive, lighting up her Diwali with the warmth of friendship and companionship.

During the Diwali vacation, Lily found herself with a rare day off from work, yet she couldn't shake the feeling of loneliness that crept in whenever she had time to spare. With Surya away in his hometown, she felt a twinge of emptiness, yearning for his presence even though she knew he was miles away.

As she scrolled through Surya's Instagram feed, each picture served as a bittersweet reminder of his absence. With every glance, she couldn't help but wonder what he was doing at that very moment. Was he celebrating Diwali with his family? Was he enjoying the festivities with friends? The uncertainty gnawed at her, leaving her feeling restless and anxious.

Unable to resist the urge to reach out, Lily decided to send Surya a message, her fingers hesitating over the keys as she typed out a simple inquiry: "When are you coming back?" She hit send, hoping for a quick response that would alleviate her growing sense of unease.

Minutes turned into hours, yet no reply came. Lily found herself glued to her phone, checking it every few minutes in hopes of seeing a notification from Surya. But as the hours passed with no response, her mind began to wander down a darker path.

Thoughts of Surya spending time with another girl in his hometown clouded Lily's mind, filling her with a sense of insecurity and jealousy she couldn't shake. Each passing moment only intensified her feelings of loneliness, leaving her feeling more isolated than ever before.

Lost in her thoughts, Lily couldn't escape the nagging doubts that plagued her mind. What if Surya had found someone else? What if he no longer cared about their friendship? The questions swirled around her, casting a shadow over what should have been a joyous holiday.

As the day wore on, Lily found herself retreating further into her own thoughts, her mind consumed by the uncertainties of her situation. With each passing hour, her anxiety grew, leaving her feeling more alone than ever before.

In the midst of her turmoil, Lily couldn't help but wish for some sign from Surya a message, anything to ease the ache of her loneliness. But as the day came to a close and darkness fell outside her window, she was left to confront her fears alone, grappling with the uncertainty of what tomorrow would bring.

After what felt like an eternity of waiting, Lily finally received a reply from Surya. Her heart skipped a beat as she read his message, relief flooding through her at the sight of his name on her screen. He apologized for not responding sooner, explaining that he had been caught up in the busyness of his Diwali celebrations back home.

Mixed emotions surged within Lily as she read his words. On one hand, she was overjoyed to hear from him after what had felt like an eternity of waiting. But on the other hand, a flicker of annoyance flared within her at the thought of him being too busy to reply to her earlier message.

Despite her conflicting feelings, Lily knew she couldn't stay angry with Surya for long. After all, he had taken the time to reach out to her now, and that was all that mattered. With a sigh, she pushed aside her lingering frustrations and typed out a response, expressing her understanding of his situation and her relief at hearing from him again.

As the days passed, Lily and Surya continued to exchange messages, their conversations ranging from casual inquiries about each other's well-being to playful banter and lighthearted exchanges. Each message brought a smile to Lily's face, as she savored the connection she shared with Surya, no matter how fleeting it may be.

Despite the physical distance between them, Lily found solace in their virtual interactions, finding comfort in the knowledge that Surya was just a message away. And as she drifted off to sleep each night, her thoughts were filled with visions of him, his messages echoing in her mind like a sweet lullaby, soothing her troubled thoughts and lulling her into a peaceful slumber.

As the day of Surya's return to the office finally arrived, Lily couldn't contain her excitement. She arrived at the office bright and early, her heart aflutter with anticipation. As she settled into her workstation, she found herself stealing glances at the entrance, eagerly awaiting Surya's arrival.

Before long, Surya walked through the office doors, his presence immediately drawing Lily's attention. Their eyes met briefly as he made his way to his desk, and a small smile tugged at the corners of Lily's lips as she greeted him with a polite hello.

"Good morning," Surya replied with a nod, returning her greeting in kind. Despite the bubbling excitement that simmered beneath the surface, their interactions remained formal and restrained, both of them hesitant to reveal the depth of their emotions.

As they settled into their respective tasks for the day, Lily found it difficult to focus, her mind wandering back to the moments they had shared in the past. She stole glances at Surya whenever she thought he wasn't looking, admiring the way the sunlight danced across his features and the focused intensity with which he approached his work.

Despite their shared anticipation, the air between them remained tinged with a sense of restraint, neither of them willing to take the first step towards breaking down the barriers that separated them. Instead, they buried themselves in their work, their minds preoccupied with thoughts of what could be.

Hours passed in a blur as they immersed themselves in their tasks, the occasional exchange of brief greetings serving as the only interruptions in their shared silence. Yet beneath the surface, a current of unspoken tension lingered, their unspoken feelings simmering just beneath the surface.

As the day drew to a close and their colleagues began to trickle out of the office, Lily found herself stealing one last glance at Surya before gathering her belongings and preparing to leave. Despite the lack of overt interaction between them, she couldn't shake the feeling of warmth that blossomed within her at the sight of him.

With a final nod of farewell, Lily bid Surya good night, a small smile playing at her lips as she made her way towards the exit. Though their interactions had been briefing and restrained, she couldn't help but feel a glimmer of hope stirring within her chest, a silent promise of what the future might hold.

Feeling hurt and confused by Surya's sudden change in behavior, Lily couldn't help but wonder what she had done wrong. She had grown accustomed to their regular exchanges on Instagram, finding comfort in the familiarity of their conversations. But now, faced with his silence, she felt a pang of sadness gnaw at her heart.

Summoning the courage to confront him, Lily mustered the strength to send him a message, asking why he had been ignoring her. When his response came, explaining that he needed space due to family reasons, Lily felt a wave of disappointment wash over her. She had hoped for a different explanation, one that would assuage her fears and uncertainties.

Despite the hurt she felt, Lily knew that she had to respect Surya's wishes. Reluctantly, she replied with a simple "ok," masking the turmoil raging within her. Deep down, she longed to reach out to him, to plead with him to reconsider, but she knew that giving him space was the right thing to do.

In the days that followed, Lily found herself grappling with a whirlwind of emotions. She missed their conversations, the easy banter and shared moments of laughter. Yet, she knew that she had to give Surya the space he needed, no matter how difficult it was for her.

With each passing day, Lily found herself growing stronger, slowly coming to terms with the reality of their situation. She focused on her work, throwing herself into her routines in an effort to distract herself from the ache in her heart.

Lily was determined to keep her distance, her resolve unyielding despite the ache in her heart. As Surya's gaze lingered on her, she steadfastly refused to meet his eyes, her own gaze fixed resolutely on her work.

When a doubt arose in her spreadsheet, Lily hesitated to approach Surya for help, choosing instead to seek assistance from a colleague who seated beside Surya. She couldn't bring herself to break the barrier she had erected between them, even as her heart longed for reconciliation.

Lily: (internal monologue) "I can't let him see how much he affects me. Not after everything that's happened.

Surya: (to himself) "Why won't she look at me? What did I do wrong?"

As the rain began to pour, the air grew colder, sending chills down Surya's spine. Despite the warmth of the room, the cool breeze from the ceiling fan caused him to shiver involuntarily. Lily couldn't help but notice the slight tremor in Surya's frame, a pang of guilt tugging at her heartstrings.

Lily: (hesitantly) "Should I switch off fan... No, I can't. Not after what happened."

Surya: (to himself, shivering) "It's so cold in here. But I can't ask her to turn off the fan."

Throughout the day, Lily wrestled with her conscience, torn between her desire to reach out to Surya and her determination to maintain her distance.

As the hours passed, Lily's resolve began to falter, her heart yearning for reconciliation even as her pride held her back.

Lily: (sighing) "Maybe... No, I can't. But what if..."

But just as Lily began to entertain the possibility of breaking the ice, a message from Surya appeared on her phone, his words a lifeline in the sea of uncertainty.

Surya: (texting) "Hey, is everything okay? You seem distant today."

Lily's heart skipped a beat as she read his message, her emotions swirling in a whirlwind of conflicting desires.

Lily: (replying, with a hint of defiance) "I'm fine. Just busy with work."

Surya: (responding, earnestly) "I miss talking to you. Can we please talk like we used to?"

As Lily read his words, a sense of warmth flooded her being, thawing the walls she had erected around her heart.

Lily: (smiling to herself) "Maybe... Just maybe, we can find our way back to each other."

As she read his messages, a wave of relief washed over her, dispelling the clouds of doubt and uncertainty that had plagued her in recent days. With each word, Surya breathed new life into their fractured connection, offering Lily a glimmer of hope for the future.

In that moment, Lily knew that she had found her way back to Surya, their bond stronger and more resilient than ever before. And as they exchanged messages late into the night, Lily allowed herself to bask in the glow of their renewed connection, grateful for the opportunity to once again share in the warmth of Surya's presence.

With each passing night, Lily found herself immersed in a world of endless conversation with Surya, their exchanges weaving a web of joy and excitement around her. Late into the night, their messages danced across the screen, carrying with them the weight of their shared dreams and aspirations.

Lily: (typing eagerly) "I can't stop smiling whenever I talk to you. It's like you have this magic power over me."

Surya: (responding with equal enthusiasm) "Believe me, the feeling is mutual. You bring so much light into my life."

Every word from Surya was like a melody to Lily's ears, each message bringing a blush to her cheeks that she couldn't hide, no matter how hard she tried.

Roommate 1: (noticing Lily's radiant expression) "Who got you glowing like a firefly? You've been glued to your phone all night."

Lily: (trying to play it cool) "Oh, just catching up with a friend. You know how it is."

But her roommates sensed there was more to Lily's happiness than she was letting on. They prodded her gently, eager to unravel the mystery behind her newfound joy.

Roommate 2: (teasingly) "Come on, spill the beans! Who's the lucky person making you blush like that?"

Lily: (giggling nervously) "Oh, it's nothing. Just some late-night chats with a friend."

Despite her attempts to keep Surya a secret, Lily couldn't contain the boundless joy he brought into her life. Each night spent in conversation with him was like a treasure trove of happiness, filling her heart with warmth and her soul with an indescribable sense of contentment.

Despite their deep affection for each other, Lily and Surya hesitated to express their feelings openly. They danced around the topic, their hearts yearning for a love they both knew existed but were afraid to acknowledge.

Surya: (tentatively) "Lily, I need to tell you something. My family is pressuring me to find a match. They've even sent me a picture of a girl they think would be suitable."

Lily's heart sank at the thought of Surya being matched with someone else, but she forced a smile and replied, "She looks nice. You should consider her."

Surya: (sensing Lily's discomfort) "But honestly, Lily, I'm not sure if I'm ready for marriage. I don't feel a connection with her like I do with you."

Lily's heart skipped a beat at his words, a glimmer of hope flickering within her. She dared to ask, "What kind of girl are you looking for then?"

Surya: (with a smile) "Someone exactly like you, Lily. Someone who understands me, who shares my interests and values."

Lily couldn't contain the flutter of excitement in her chest, but she remained composed on the surface. "Well, no one will ever be exactly like me," she teased, trying to mask her true feelings.

Surya: (playfully) "True, but do you have any sisters who might like you exactly?"

Lily's heart swelled with affection at his words. "I don't have any sisters, but I can certainly keep an eye out for a girl who meets your criteria," she replied, her voice tinged with a mixture of happiness and longing.

Their conversation continued late into the night, each message exchanged bringing them closer together, even as they tiptoed around the unspoken truth of their love for each other.

One evening, Lily and her friend Sneha decided to try beer for the first time in their lives. With no one else in their room, they seized the opportunity to indulge in a girls' night in. Sneha enlisted her boyfriend to procure two beers for them, and they set about creating the perfect ambiance for their evening. The room was adorned with roses, snacks were laid out on the table, and they even had special dresses for the occasion.

As they cracked open their beers and settled in, the atmosphere became relaxed and carefree. Lily, feeling emboldened by the alcohol, decided to reach out to Surya via Instagram. Fingers flying over her phone screen, she typed out her message, her curiosity getting the better of her.

Lily: Hey Surya, quick question... Have you ever had a girlfriend before?

The response came quickly, and Lily's heart sank as she read Surya's reply.

Surya: Yeah, I have. But it didn't work out. She got married to someone else eventually.

Lily felt a twinge of sadness at the news but brushed it off, determined not to let it ruin their evening. Buoyed by the liquid courage coursing through her veins, she decided to take a leap of faith and confess her feelings to Surya.

Lily: You know, Surya, I've been thinking... I kinda like you.

Surya: Oh, okay.

Lily's heart skipped a beat at Surya's casual response, but she pressed on, feeling emboldened by the alcohol.

Lily: And I... I really want to kiss you. On the cheek, I mean.

Surya: Lily, you're drinking beer right now. Maybe it's best to sleep it off. You might regret saying all this in the morning.

But Lily was undeterred, her confidence unwavering in the face of Surya's caution.

Lily: No, Surya, I won't regret it. I'll delete this chat tomorrow so I won't even remember. Trust me.

With that, Lily put her phone down and turned her attention back to Sneha, the warmth of the alcohol enveloping her in a blissful haze.

Hours passed, and Lily eventually succumbed to sleep, her dreams filled with thoughts of Surya. And as she drifted off, her phone lay forgotten by her side, the messages exchanged between her and Surya serving as a silent reminder of the night's events.

The morning after their late-night exchange, Lily woke up feeling a mixture of guilt and awkwardness. As she scrolled through her phone, the memories of her conversation with Surya flooded back, and she couldn't help but feel a twinge of regret. Glancing across the office, she caught Surya's eye, and for a moment, their gazes locked in silent acknowledgment of the shared secret between them.

But to Lily's surprise, Surya seemed unfazed by the events of the previous night. His Instagram messages were casual and friendly, as if nothing out of the ordinary had occurred. His easygoing demeanor put Lily at ease, and she found herself relaxing into the familiar routine of their workday.

As they went about their respective tasks, Lily and Surya exchanged occasional glances, each one carrying a silent understanding of the bond that had formed between them. Despite the lingering sense of awkwardness, their shared moments of connection served as a reminder that their relationship was built on more than just one late night conversation.

ﭖﭖﭖ

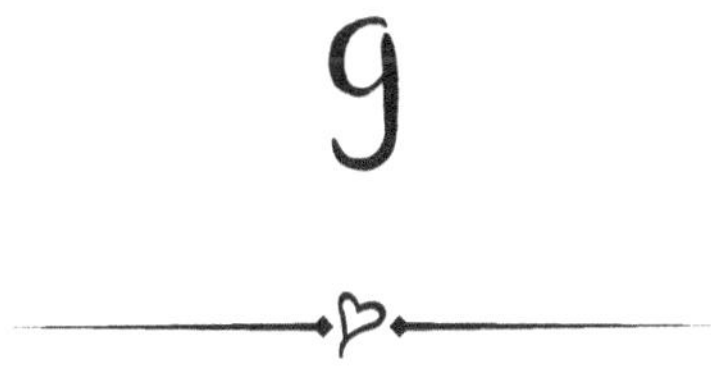

Unexpected Connections

Every night, like clockwork, Lily and Surya found solace in their Instagram chats. Their conversations were a tapestry of thoughts, dreams, and aspirations, weaving together the fabric of their growing bond. They talked about everything under the sun from work-related challenges to personal ambitions and the intricacies of life itself.

Their discussions often stretched into the late hours of the night, as they delved into topics ranging from their career aspirations to their deepest desires. Lily found herself opening up to Surya in ways she hadn't with anyone else, sharing her hopes and fears with a vulnerability that surprised even her.

Through their nightly exchanges, Lily and Surya discovered a deep connection that transcended the boundaries of their professional relationship. They became each other's confidants, supporting and encouraging one another through life's ups and downs.

As their friendship blossomed, Lily and Surya found comfort in each other's words, finding solace in the knowledge that no matter what challenges lay ahead, they had each other to lean on.

As the days turned into nights, Lily and Surya found themselves delving deeper into their relationship. One night, while immersed in their late-night chat, the topic of marriage arose. Lily, feeling a surge of emotions, tentatively asked Surya, "Shall we get married now, at this moment?"

Surya's heart skipped a beat as he read her message. After a moment's pause, he replied with unwavering certainty, "Yes, we can get married."

The idea of an Instagram chat wedding seemed surreal yet strangely appealing to them. They both agreed that Instagram, their digital sanctuary, would be the perfect venue for their union. Without any hesitation, they decided on a date and time – 20th December 2019 at 12:33 AM – to exchange their vows and declare themselves husband and wife.

As the clock struck midnight on the appointed day, Lily and Surya eagerly awaited the moment that would forever change their lives. With hearts pounding and excitement coursing through their veins, they exchanged heartfelt messages, professing their love and devotion to each other.

"Lily, I've always wanted you as my wife, and now you are," Surya confessed, his words brimming with joy and affection.

Overwhelmed with happiness, Lily responded, "I feel like the luckiest woman alive to have you as my husband, Surya. I'm so happy to be yours."

In the virtual realm of Instagram, surrounded by their digital friends and followers, Lily and Surya exchanged vows, promising to love and cherish each other for eternity. Though they were apart physically, their love knew no bounds, transcending the limitations of time and space.

After their impromptu Instagram wedding, Lily and Surya spent the rest of the night chatting and basking in the glow of their newfound marital bliss. Each message exchanged between them was filled with love, laughter, and dreams of their future together.

"I can't believe we're married," Lily exclaimed, her heart brimming with happiness. "I feel like the luckiest woman in the world."

Surya echoed her sentiments, expressing his gratitude for having Lily by his side. "Life has given me its best gift – you," he said, his words filled with warmth and sincerity.

As the night drew to a close, Lily and Surya bid each other goodnight, their hearts overflowing with love and gratitude. Though they were miles apart, they felt closer than ever before, united in their love and commitment to each other.

As they drifted off to sleep, their minds filled with thoughts of their shared future, Lily and Surya knew that their Instagram wedding was just the beginning of their beautiful journey together.

With their virtual wedding sealing their bond, Lily and Surya's love blossomed even more. Surya, feeling the weight of their newfound commitment, expressed his love openly, sending Lily heartfelt messages like "I love you, Lily." Now you are my wife so I have right to say I love you right. Lily couldn't help but blush at his sweet words, feeling the warmth of his affection wash over her.

Their Instagram chat became their sanctuary, a place where they could express their love freely without any limitations. They found solace in each other's words, chatting throughout the day and night, their conversations filled with laughter, affection, and dreams for the future.

Despite the distance separating them, seeing each other's faces on their screens brought them immense joy, making them feel as though they were right beside each other. Lily and Surya's love knew no bounds, transcending the digital realm and filling their hearts with happiness and contentment.

Despite being physically apart during, Lily and Surya's hearts remained intertwined, tethered by the invisible threads of love and affection. Whenever Surya had to step out for work, he couldn't help but miss Lily's presence by his side. Even after the allotted time had passed, he would return to the office just to catch a glimpse of her, his heart swelling with joy at the sight of her.

For Lily, knowing that Surya cared enough to seek her out, even in his absence, filled her with a sense of warmth and happiness. His unwavering attention and concern made her feel cherished and loved, despite the physical distance between them.

Their bond transcended the confines of their workplace, extending into the depths of their souls. Surya longed to be the first person Lily saw when she entered the office, and the last one she bid farewell to at the end of the day. Likewise, Lily found solace in Surya's presence, his absence leaving a void that only his return could fill.

Their connection was a testament to the power of love, proving that distance was no match for the depth of their feelings. Though separated by space and time, Lily and Surya's hearts remained forever entwined, their love enduring and unwavering in the face of any obstacle.

After their customary nightly stroll around the PG premises, Lily mustered up the courage to ask Surya for a handshake. With a playful grin, Surya obliged, his hand meeting Lily's in a brief yet meaningful gesture of camaraderie. The warmth of their touch lingered long after they parted ways, leaving both Lily and Surya with a sense of contentment and joy.

As Surya made his way back home, his heart danced with delight at the memory of their handshake. He couldn't help but text Lily, jesting that he would never wash his hand again, relishing in the lingering connection they shared. Lily, too, felt a surge of happiness at the thought of their brief but significant encounter, her heart skipping a beat at Surya's playful message.

Later that evening, as they chatted on Instagram, their conversation flowed effortlessly, each message carrying with it the echoes of their shared moment. Though their interaction was brief, the memory of their handshake lingered in their hearts, a testament to the special bond they shared.

As Lily and Surya chatted on Instagram, their conversation took a daring turn. They decided that they wanted to feel each other's presence more intimately, and Surya expressed his desire to hug Lily. Excitement mingled with nervousness as they agreed to meet the next day in the lift for their clandestine embrace.

The following day arrived, and Lily and Surya found themselves standing side by side in the lift, their hearts pounding with anticipation. However, as the doors closed and the lift began to ascend, tension hung heavy in the air, making it difficult for either of them to make the first move. Time seemed to stretch as they exchanged furtive glances, unable to bridge the gap between them.

With only 45 seconds until they reached their floor, Lily and Surya realized that their first attempt at a hug had been unsuccessful. Disappointed yet determined, they silently vowed to try again.

Back at their respective desks in the office, Lily and Surya exchanged messages, reassuring each other that they would not give up. Their determination fueled their resolve, and they eagerly awaited their next opportunity to share a hug.

When the moment finally arrived, and they found themselves once again alone in the lift, Lily and Surya's hearts beat in unison as they drew closer to each other. This time, with a surge of courage, they enveloped each other in a warm embrace, feeling the electricity of their connection course through their veins.

The embrace was fleeting yet profound, a silent acknowledgment of the bond they shared. As they parted ways and returned to their respective workstations, Lily and Surya carried with them the memory of their secret hug, a cherished moment that bound them together in a deeper, more intimate way.

As Lily and Surya continued their conversations on Instagram, their discussions grew more intimate. They shared their feelings about their previous hug and decided that they wanted to take their connection to the next level they wanted to kiss each other.

The following day, Lily and Surya arrived at the office early, their hearts racing with anticipation. They met at the lift, where tension hung thick in the air. As they stepped inside, Surya gently cupped Lily's face in his hands and leaned in to kiss her lips.

For 40 seconds, time stood still as their lips met in a tender, yet electrifying embrace. When the lift doors finally opened, Lily quietly made her way to her desk, her mind a whirlwind of emotions: happiness, excitement, and a hint of anxiety. As she stole a glance at Surya's desk, their eyes met, silently acknowledging the shared moment between them.

Later, Surya reached out to Lily, asking if she was okay. Their chat provided a sense of reassurance and comfort, marking the end of a day filled with both excitement and introspection.

Lily and Surya's clandestine encounters in the lift, their tender hugs, and evening walks in the park were moments of pure joy and bliss for both of them. Each interaction was filled with an unspoken connection, a shared understanding that transcended words.

Their lift lip kisses were fleeting yet intense, leaving them both breathless and exhilarated. In those brief moments, time seemed to stand still as they lost themselves in the warmth of each other's embrace. Their hugs, exchanged in the quiet solitude of the lift, were a source of comfort and solace, offering reassurance in the midst of their busy lives.

But it was their evening walks in the park that truly allowed them to savor each other's company. As they strolled hand in hand, surrounded by the tranquility of nature, they shared their hopes, dreams, and fears with one another. Their conversations flowed freely, weaving a tapestry of shared memories and shared aspirations.

For Lily and Surya, happiness knew no bounds in these stolen moments of togetherness. In each other's presence, they found a sense of completeness and fulfillment that they had never experienced before. Their love blossomed in the quiet corners of their hearts, growing stronger with each passing day.

As they continued to share their thoughts, feelings, and dreams, their bond deepened, forging a connection that was as profound as it was beautiful. And though their love story unfolded in secret, hidden from the prying eyes of the world, its beauty and intensity were undeniable.

In each other's arms, Lily and Surya found a sanctuary a place where they could be themselves, unburdened by the expectations of others. And as they reveled in the simple joys of their shared moments, they knew that their love was true, enduring, and everlasting.

As Lily embarked on a new journey with her job offer and the prospect of six months of training in Hyderabad, she couldn't help but feel a twinge of sadness knowing that she would be separated from Surya during this time. She shared the news with him, and his reaction mirrored her own feelings of disappointment at the impending separation.

Determined to leave Surya with a token of her affection, something to remember her by during their time apart, Lily decided to surprise him with a meaningful gift. She spent hours browsing through shops, searching for the perfect item that would convey her love and devotion.

Eventually, she found it a delicate ring, elegant in its simplicity yet imbued with profound significance. With the ring safely tucked away in her pocket, Lily arranged to meet Surya for a walk in the park that evening. The setting sun cast a warm glow over the landscape, adding a touch of magic to their rendezvous.

As they strolled along the winding paths of the park, Lily found herself stealing glances at Surya, her heart swelling with love for him. Finally, when the moment felt right, she reached into her pocket and produced the ring, presenting it to him with a shy smile.

"Surya, I want you to have this," she said softly, slipping the ring onto his finger. "It's a symbol of my love for you, something to remind you of me while we're apart."

Surya's eyes widened in surprise as he gazed down at the ring, his heart swelling with emotion. He was deeply touched by Lily's gesture, grateful for her thoughtfulness and the depth of her love for him. Taking her hand in his, he squeezed it gently, overcome with emotion.

"Lily, I don't know what to say," he murmured, his voice thick with emotion. "This means more to me than you'll ever know. I'll treasure it always."

As they continued their walk, Lily couldn't shake the feeling that there was something more she wanted to say, something she needed to express before they parted ways. And then, as if on cue, she spotted a cluster of flowers blooming by the side of the path.

Inspired by the beauty of nature surrounding them, Lily gathered a few of the blooms, carefully selecting the most vibrant and fragrant ones. With trembling hands, she held them out to Surya, her heart pounding in her chest.

"Surya, I love you," she declared, her voice trembling with emotion. "These flowers are a symbol of my love for you, a reminder that no matter where we are, my heart will always be with you."

Surya's eyes softened as he accepted the flowers from Lily, his heart swelling with love for her. Leaning in, he pressed a gentle kiss to her cheek, his lips lingering against her skin for a moment longer than necessary.

"Lily, I love you," he whispered, his voice barely above a whisper. "And I promise, no matter where you go, I'll be waiting for you with open arms when you return."

With that, they exchanged one final embrace, holding onto each other tightly as if trying to imprint the moment into their memories forever. And as they parted ways, a sense of peace washed over them, knowing that their love would endure even in the face of distance and separation.

The following day dawned with a bittersweet farewell as Lily bid her final goodbyes to her colleagues and friends at the office. There was a sense of sadness in the air as she hugged each of them tightly, knowing that she would miss their presence in her daily life. Yet, there was also an excitement bubbling within her as she prepared to embark on a new chapter of her life.

With her bags packed and her heart filled with anticipation, Lily set off for Hyderabad, ready to embrace the challenges and opportunities that awaited her in her new job training. The journey was long, but every mile brought her closer to her destination, filling her with a sense of purpose and determination.

As the train chugged along the tracks, Lily found herself lost in thought, reflecting on the journey that had brought her to this moment. She thought of Surya, the man she loved, and the ring she had given him as a token of her affection. She wondered how he was coping with her absence, if he missed her as much as she missed him.

Despite the distance between them, Lily took comfort in the knowledge that their love would endure, transcending the physical miles that separated them. She clung to the memories they had shared, the moments of laughter and joy that had filled her heart with happiness.

Arriving in Hyderabad, Lily felt a surge of excitement as she stepped off the train and onto the bustling platform. The city was alive with energy, its streets teeming with people going about their daily lives. For a moment, Lily was missing the familiar sights and sounds of her office.

But as she made her way to her new accommodation, her excitement grew, overshadowing any feelings of apprehension or doubt. She was ready to embrace this new chapter of her life, to immerse herself in her job training and make the most of this opportunity for personal and professional growth.

Settling into her new surroundings, Lily felt a sense of optimism wash over her, filling her with renewed determination and purpose. She knew that the road ahead would be challenging, but she was ready to face it head-on, fueled by the love and support of those she held dear.

And as she closed her eyes that night, her thoughts turned to Surya, the man who held her heart in his hands. Though they were miles apart, she knew that their love would only grow stronger with each passing day, binding them together in a bond that was unbreakable, no matter the distance.

As she awakens from her slumber, her first conscious thought is of Surya, his name dancing through her mind like a cherished melody. Throughout the day, he remains a constant presence in her thoughts, his image lingering in the corners of her consciousness, infusing her every moment with a sense of warmth and comfort.

And as night falls and she drifts into the realm of dreams, it is Surya who occupies the final space in her mind, his essence intertwining with her subconscious as she surrenders to the embrace of sleep. From dawn till dusk, and from dusk till dawn, he is the unwavering anchor of her thoughts, the embodiment of her deepest desires and fondest hopes.

During the six-month duration of Lily's job training in Hyderabad, she and Surya found solace in their frequent conversations over the phone, Instagram chats, and video calls. Despite the physical distance between them, their bond only grew stronger as they navigated the challenges of being apart.

Their phone calls would often stretch into the late hours of the night, as they exchanged stories about their day, shared their dreams and aspirations, and whispered words of love and affection. Each conversation felt like a lifeline, bridging the gap between them and reaffirming their connection despite the miles that separated them.

On Instagram, they would exchange messages throughout the day, sending each other photos, memes, and heartfelt messages that brought smiles to their faces and warmth to their hearts. It was their digital sanctuary, a place where they could express their love and longing for each other freely and openly.

And when words were not enough, they turned to video calls, relishing the opportunity to see each other's faces and hear each other's voices in real-time. The distance melted away as they laughed together, shared intimate moments, and basked in the comfort of each other's presence, if only through a screen.

But amidst the joy of their virtual encounters, there was also a lingering sense of longing and yearning. They missed each other deeply, craving the physical closeness and intimacy that could only be found in each other's arms. Yet, they knew that their separation was temporary, a necessary step on their journey towards a future together.

And so, they held onto each other tightly, cherishing every moment they spent together, whether in person or through a screen. For in their love, they found strength, resilience, and the unwavering belief that no matter the distance, they would always find their way back to each other.

ᑭᑭᑭ

10

Birthday Trip

As Lily's birthday approached, Surya found himself grappling with the distance that separated them. Determined to make her special day memorable despite the miles between them, he racked his brain for the perfect gift that would bring a smile to her face.

After careful consideration, Surya settled on a plan that he hoped would exceed Lily's expectations. He remembered her once mentioning her dream of visiting the beach, an experience she had yet to have in her lifetime. With this in mind, he made the bold decision to whisk her away to Goa, a coastal paradise renowned for its sandy shores and azure waters. Goa, often dubbed as India's beach capital, is a coastal paradise located on the western coast of India. Renowned for its stunning sandy beaches, vibrant culture, and pulsating nightlife, Goa attracts tourists from around the globe. From the lively shores of Baga and Calangute to the serene stretches of Palolem and Agonda, each beach in Goa offers a unique experience. Beyond its beaches, Goa boasts a rich heritage reflected in its colonial architecture, ancient temples, and bustling markets. Visitors can explore historic churches like the Basilica of Bom Jesus and delve into the state's Portuguese past in the charming streets of Panaji and Old Goa. With its eclectic mix of sun, sand, and spirituality, Goa promises an unforgettable getaway for every traveler.

With meticulous attention to detail, Surya set about planning the trip, ensuring that every aspect was tailored to Lily's preferences. He booked his ticket to Hyderabad, where Lily was undergoing her job training, intending to surprise her in person. Once there, he revealed his grand plan to take her on a getaway to Goa, promising her an unforgettable adventure.

When Lily learned of Surya's surprise, her heart swelled with joy and gratitude. The prospect of embarking on their first trip together filled her with excitement and anticipation, and she eagerly packed her bags in preparation for the journey ahead.

As they set off for Goa together, the air was filled with anticipation, and their hearts beat in unison with the rhythm of the train as it carried them towards their destination.

Throughout the journey, Surya regaled Lily with tales of their upcoming adventure, painting vivid pictures of the sun-kissed beaches, the vibrant culture, and the countless memories they would create together. Lily listened intently, her eyes shining with excitement, as she envisioned the paradise that awaited them.

As the train rumbled on through the night, Lily and Surya found solace in each other's company, reveling in the simple pleasure of being together. They shared stories, laughter, and quiet moments of reflection, savoring the precious time they had in each other's presence.

For Surya, seeing Lily's face light up with happiness was the greatest gift of all. As they neared their destination, he felt a sense of satisfaction knowing that he had succeeded in bringing joy to the woman he loved. And for Lily, the journey to Goa was not just a trip, but a testament to the depth of Surya's love and devotion.

As they stepped off the train and onto the platform in Goa, hand in hand, they knew that their adventure was only just beginning. With hearts full of love and excitement, they set out to explore the wonders of this magical place, eager to create memories that would last a lifetime.

Upon arriving in Goa, Lily and Surya wasted no time in immersing themselves in the beauty of Baga beach. With the private resort Surya had booked, they were greeted by a stunning ambiance that left Lily in awe. The air was filled with the salty scent of the sea, and the sound of crashing waves provided the perfect soundtrack to their getaway.

After settling into their accommodations and indulging in a delicious meal, Lily couldn't contain her excitement as they made their way to the beach. The sight of the vast expanse of sand and sea filled her with pure joy, and she wasted no time in kicking off her shoes and frolicking in the waves. Surya watched on, his heart swelling with happiness at the sight of Lily's unbridled joy.

As the evening approached, they ventured into the local markets, exploring the vibrant array of goods on offer. Lily seized the opportunity to pick out a special surprise for Surya, determined to make their time together even more memorable.

Lily vanished into the sanctuary of their room, where a sense of anticipation lingered in the air. Moments later, she emerged, a vision of elegance and grace, draped in a mesmerizing black saree that accentuated her every curve. Her hair, flowing like cascading waves, framed her delicate features, adding to her ethereal allure.

Surya stood transfixed, his gaze captivated by her radiant presence. His heart swelled with admiration as he beheld her beauty, a sight that stirred something deep within him. In that moment, time seemed to stand still, the world around them fading into insignificance as they became lost in each other's gaze.

The subtle play of moonlight danced upon Lily's features, casting a soft glow that illuminated her from within. Every movement she made seemed to carry an air of enchantment, captivating Surya's senses and igniting a fire within his soul.

In Lily's presence, he found solace and serenity, a sense of completeness that he had never known before. And as they shared a tender embrace, he knew deep in his heart that this moment would be etched in his memory forever, a testament to the enduring power of love.

Their evening was spent in a romantic embrace, as they dined under the starry sky, the soft glow of candlelight casting a warm glow over their table. They savored each moment together, sharing stories, laughter, and tender gazes as they reveled in the magic of their love.

Under the twinkling stars, with the gentle sound of the waves as their backdrop and the soft music playing in the background, Lily and Surya found themselves lost in each other's company, their hearts overflowing with love and gratitude for the precious moments they shared.

As the cool breeze gently caressed their skin, Surya's lips met Lily's in a tender kiss, igniting a spark that set their hearts ablaze.

The sensation of his lips against hers sent a rush of warmth coursing through Lily's veins, her pulse quickening in tandem with the gentle rhythm of the waves. In that fleeting moment, time seemed to stand still, the world around them fading into insignificance as they surrendered to the magic of their connection.

With a soft smile, Surya whispered, "You look stunning in that black saree, Lily. Like a silhouette against the night sky, radiant and enchanting." His words, filled with genuine admiration and affection, stirred something deep within Lily's heart, filling her with a sense of joy and contentment.

As they toasted to their love and the adventures that lay ahead, Lily knew that this night would be etched in her memory forever. And as they danced beneath the moonlight, their souls intertwined, they knew that their love would only continue to grow stronger with each passing day.

As they basked in the beauty of the night, the sound of their shared laughter mingled with the symphony of the sea, creating a melody that echoed the harmony of their souls. In that moment, surrounded by the serenity of nature and the warmth of each other's presence, Surya and Lily found solace in the simplicity of their love, their hearts united as one beneath the starlit sky.

During their time in Goa, Lily and Surya embarked on thrilling adventures together, exploring the picturesque landscapes on the back of a rented bike. As they rode through the winding roads, the warm raindrops danced upon their skin, adding to the sense of exhilaration that filled the air.

With Lily nestled behind him on the bike, Surya felt a surge of joy course through him, relishing in the feeling of having her close by his side. Together, they ventured into the heart of Goa, indulging in delectable local cuisine, scouring the bustling markets for trinkets and treasures, and basking in the tranquil beauty of Goa's pristine beaches.

Surya couldn't resist capturing the magic of their journey on camera, snapping countless pictures of Lily as she laughed, danced, and reveled in the joy of their shared experiences. Each photograph was a testament to their happiness, their love radiating brightly in every frame.

On Lily's birthday, as they sat together in their cozy resort room overlooking the serene beauty of Baga beach, Surya reached into his pocket and pulled out a delicate envelope. With a gentle smile, he handed it to Lily, her eyes twinkling with curiosity and anticipation.

Lily's heart skipped a beat as she took the envelope from Surya's hand, her fingers trembling slightly with excitement. With bated breath, she carefully opened it, revealing a beautifully handwritten love letter nestled inside. Her eyes scanned the words penned by Surya, each sentence filled with heartfelt emotion and genuine affection.

My Dear Love Lily

Happy Birthday My Queen

Happy birthday to my beautiful and sweetest wife, I don't even know where to begin, I wish I could explain in word how much I love and I miss you. I have so much felt and love for you in my heart and Iwant to tell you that how much I love you. So, I decided to write a letter to you on this special day. I don'tknow how to write a letter but I just tried to express my feelings through words with little help of googletranslator. As you know your husband is dumb in studies and don't know English. Might be there is many ways to say I love you and expressing feeling, but only one way to prove it that is by actions, how I treatyou, how I behave with you, how I respect you. So, when you will be with me you will get to know how much I love you and I want you.

You are my first thought in the morning when I open my eyes and when I go to the bed you are the last thought. I always think about you. I love everything about you Lily, the way you hold me, I love when youlean your head on my shoulder, your presence makes me so much happy and I feel complete with you, I lovehow you smile when I see you, I love the way you kiss me, I will never forget the way kissed me very deeply, it was so special for me and that feeling will always remain in mind. I love how you get jealous, the way you care for me, the way you love me infinite and unconditionally, the way you want me badly, I love how Iam important for you, I love how we talk about being together forever I really love everything about you Lily, You, your eyes, your smile, your laugh, your presence just every little thing about you. You are sosmart, funny and amazing. I love you endlessly. You will be the queen of my heart, and nothing will come between us. We are going to be forever. I am truly, madly and <u>*deeply in love*</u> *with you, every day I am lovingyou more and more, you are so kind and cute my doll and I am not that foolish to let you go from out of mylife no matter what happen. You are only mine and you will be always mine. I will always love you as I haveever done. The love you have given me is so special, you made me the happiest person the day you came intomy life.*

*Do you know many times I looks at you and think to myself "How lucky I Am?" what I did that you got me, really after having you I became luckiest man on this earth, how we met, how it's started, eventhough I never thought you will become mine but I always wanted to make you mine, somewhere deep inside in my heart I had feelings for you, I never thought you will love me this much even though you were lovingme from starting. Chatting with you, talking with you and spending time with you it's a great experience andfeeling for me. You gave me beautiful and unforgettable memories. The feeling that you are in my life makes me very happy. You are too good more than I think, you are everything to me kalu **"Tumhari ek muskurahat mere saare gham mittha deti hain."** and it's* *really true. Your one text makes me so much happy. As you well aware about my behavior I have an anger issue but your one text makes me so calm, happy and stress-free. You are my medicine. you know how moody I am If I get frustrate or if am stressedstill, I will not tell things clearly and keep with me in my mind but you always there for me and makes me feel good and help me to take decision. You help me to make me better. You understand me better. Thankyou for being there always for me, I love you so much.*

I want to share my future with you, I want to love you all the day of my life, I want to express myfeeling for you, I want to make kids with you, I want to grow and old with you, I want to live and enjoy life'severy moment with you, I want everything with you what we dreamed together. Now living my life without you will be meaningless, because I almost dreamed and planned my life with you. I love you; I love you so much. You are the only thing I desire at all the times and I want to keep with me forever. I want you to bewith me forever. I never want to see you sad. I can do or I can be anything to make you smile because youand your love is everything to me. I will love you and take care of you as much I can. Sometimes I become mad and do many foolish things and made you cry, hurt you badly and now also I really have regret forwhat I did. I hurt a person whom I love most. Trust me I never want to hurt you, never ever. So please forgiveme Lily. I love you forever and I will never leave your side if I am with you or nor doesn't matter. I promise.

Whatever time we spent together it's really so memorable and special for me. We went some placesand that places become my favorite, because our memories are associated with those places. We went to park SAI temple and ISKON temple when I am with you, I don't want to pass that time. We used to walk on our favorite road, whenever I come for walk or meet you, I never want to go back, whenever I am with you,I wish this time would stop there. I love to look at you, be with you and I want to spend endless time with you. Spending time with you is the undoubtedly best thing ever. But now it been months I didn't even seeyou; I didn't touch you. When we are apart, every second every minute I spent waiting to see you again. Still,I am waiting to see you and you keep making me wait. But its ok I can wait for you. I love you, and I missyou so much, now I can't wait to see you, please come soon baby.

All I want is you and your love, please be with me forever. I am completely addicted to you, falling in love with you is the best thing that ever happened in my life and I want to fall in love with you deeperand deeper.

I want you to have a memory of my words and my feelings, so I decided to write a letter and onceyou also told me that write a letter what you feel about me so I just tried.

Even though you're not besides me right now, but you are always in my mind, I can feel you, but Ireally wish I could be with you right now holding your hand kissing you on cheeks and wish you happybirthday baby. Kiss you, Lily.

There are many things and many feelings I want to say and express, but for now I will stop hereotherwise this letter could become a book. I know you love to read books but I am not writer. Thank you so much for being the queen of my heart and filling my life with full of happiness and joy. I really can'timagine my day without you even though you're far away right now, I can feel you right next to me. Missingyou so much.

Once again happy birthday my dear.

I love you so much Lily.

Your Loving Husband

Surya.

As Lily read each line, her heart swelled with love, her eyes misting with tears of joy. Surya's words spoke directly to her soul, expressing his deepest feelings and unwavering devotion. In his letter, he poured out his love for her, recounting the countless ways she had touched his life and filled his world with light and happiness.

With each word, Lily felt a warmth spread through her, enveloping her in a cocoon of love and tenderness. Surya's love letter was a precious gift, a treasure trove of memories and promises that she would cherish forever.

As she reached the end of the letter, Lily looked up at Surya, her eyes sparkling with gratitude and love. Without uttering a single word, she threw her arms around him, pulling him into a tight embrace. In that moment, surrounded by the soft glow of candlelight and the soothing sound of ocean waves, Lily knew that she was exactly where she was meant to be in Surya's arms, enveloped in his love.

Their bond grew stronger with each passing moment, their love deepening with every shared experience. As Lily held Surya close, she whispered a silent vow – to cherish their love, to nurture their relationship, and to treasure every precious moment they shared together.

With Surya by her side, Lily felt truly blessed, knowing that their love would guide them through whatever challenges life may bring. Hand in hand, they embarked on the journey of a lifetime, their hearts intertwined in a love that was destined to last forever.

As they explored Goa hand in hand, Lily and Surya found themselves immersed in the sheer bliss of the moment, their hearts overflowing with love and gratitude for each other's company. They were the epitome of a happy couple, their smiles lighting up the world around them as they forged unforgettable memories together.

After three unforgettable days in Goa, it was time for Lily and Surya to bid farewell to the coastal paradise and return to Hyderabad. Though they were sad to leave behind the beauty of Goa, they knew that they carried with them the cherished moments they had shared, memories that would last a lifetime.

As they said their goodbyes and boarded the plane back home, Lily and Surya knew that their journey together was far from over. With hearts full of love and adventure, they looked forward to the countless adventures that awaited them, knowing that as long as they had each other, every moment would be filled with joy and happiness. They arrived at their respective places and back into their daily life.

As the last month of Lily's training drew near, she found herself faced with an important decision where would she begin her career? Her manager presented her with a list of cities to choose from, and without hesitation, Lily knew exactly where she wanted to go. Indore – Surya's hometown and soon-to-be her own.

Excitement bubbled within Lily as she imagined starting this new chapter of her life in a city so dear to Surya's heart. She shared her decision with Surya, her eyes sparkling with anticipation, and his joy mirrored hers. Knowing that they would soon be together in Indore filled them both with an indescribable happiness.

As Lily bid farewell to her colleagues and friends at her training institute, she carried with her a sense of anticipation mixed with a tinge of melancholy. Yet, beneath it all, there was an overwhelming sense of hope: the hope of a future filled with endless possibilities, shared dreams, and unwavering love.

ﬗﬗﬗ

From Distant Hearts to Close Connections

As the days passed, Lily made the necessary arrangements for her move to Indore. With Surya's unwavering support and guidance, she found a comfortable PG accommodation and began to settle into her new surroundings. Surya was by her side every step of the way, his love and encouragement serving as a source of strength during this transition.

Indore, located in the heart of India in the state of Madhya Pradesh, is a bustling city known for its rich cultural heritage, historical significance, and vibrant atmosphere. As the largest city in Madhya Pradesh, Indore is a major commercial and industrial hub, renowned for its thriving textile and manufacturing industries. The city boasts a unique blend of traditional and modern elements, with ancient temples and palaces standing alongside contemporary skyscrapers and bustling markets. Indore is also famous for its delectable street food, offering a tantalizing array of local delicacies that attract food enthusiasts from far and wide. With its warm hospitality, vibrant festivals, and dynamic lifestyle, Indore captures the essence of India's diverse and colorful tapestry.

However, amidst the excitement of her new beginnings, a shadow of sadness lingered the prospect of once again being in a long-distance relationship weighed heavily on both Lily and Surya's hearts. Despite the distance that would separate them, they remained steadfast in their love and commitment to each other, finding solace in the knowledge that their bond was stronger than any miles that lay between them.

With Surya's love guiding her every step of the way, Lily embarked on her journey to Indore, her heart brimming with excitement and anticipation. She knew that no matter the distance, their love would always find a way to bridge the gap and keep them connected, united in their shared dreams and unwavering devotion to each other.

Despite their strong bond and affection for each other, Lily and Surya sometimes found themselves at odds over minor issues. Like any couple, they faced occasional disagreements and misunderstandings as they navigated the complexities of their relationship. These moments of tension and frustration were natural parts of their journey together, and they worked through them with patience and understanding, ultimately emerging stronger and more united than before.

However, their bond was stronger than any disagreement, and they always found a way to overcome their differences and resolve their conflicts. Through open communication, patience, and understanding, they were able to reaffirm their love for each other and move forward, their relationship strengthened by each challenge they faced together.

In an earnest attempt to close the geographical gap separating them, Surya embarked on frequent journeys from Pune to Indore, all in pursuit of precious moments spent in Lily's company. Despite the myriad obligations weighing on his shoulders and the demands of his own life, he made a steadfast commitment to nurturing their relationship, prioritizing their bond above all else. These visits were not merely fleeting encounters but rather cherished opportunities for them to bask in each other's presence, to laugh, to share, and to forge enduring memories together. Despite the physical distance that threatened to pull them apart, each visit served as a testament to their unwavering dedication and the unbreakable strength of their love.

During Surya's stays in Indore, their time together became a sanctuary, a haven where they could escape from the world and lose themselves in each other's embrace. With every step they took through the bustling streets of Indore, their fingers intertwined, their laughter dancing on the breeze, they felt as if the world around them faded into insignificance, leaving only the two of them in their own private universe.

As they shared intimate dinners beneath the twinkling canopy of stars, their conversations flowed effortlessly, each word spoken carrying the weight of their love and devotion. "I never want this moment to end," Surya whispered, his gaze fixed on Lily's radiant smile, his heart overflowing with affection. Lily, her eyes alight with adoration, reached out to caress his cheek, her touch a silent promise of eternal devotion.

In those stolen moments of togetherness, they found solace, comfort, and a sense of belonging that transcended the boundaries of time and space. Each shared glance, each tender embrace, served as a reminder of the depth of their connection and the enduring strength of their love.

And as the night deepened and the world around them faded into darkness, Surya's longing for Lily grew more intense. Unable to resist the pull of his desire, he leaned in close, his lips capturing hers in a deep, passionate kiss. Their embrace was electric, igniting a fire within them that burned with a fierce intensity. "You're the love of my life," Surya murmured between kisses, his voice husky with emotion. Lily, her heart racing with desire, responded with equal fervor, her lips meeting his in a fervent dance of love and longing.

In the sanctuary of their shared moments, Surya's every touch ignited a wildfire of sensation within Lily, sending shivers of pleasure cascading down her spine. As his fingertips traced delicate patterns across her skin, she felt herself melting into his embrace, surrendering to the intoxicating warmth of his presence.

With each whispered word and lingering gaze, Surya spoke volumes without uttering a sound, his eyes a reflection of the depth of his love and devotion. Lily found herself captivated by the tenderness in his touch, the sincerity in his voice, and the passion that burned within him like a beacon in the night.

But it was his kisses that truly transported Lily to another realm, a place where time stood still and the world faded into oblivion. With each brush of his lips against hers, she felt herself soaring to new heights of ecstasy, her heart beating in rhythm with his own.

His touch was a symphony of sensation, each caress sending ripples of pleasure coursing through her body. And as she surrendered to the euphoria of his embrace, she knew without a doubt that she was home in his arms, where she belonged.

For Surya, every kiss was a testament to the depth of his love, a declaration of his unwavering commitment to her happiness and fulfillment. And as he held her close, he whispered promises of forever, his words a soothing balm to her soul.

In those fleeting moments of intimacy, Lily knew that she was cherished beyond measure, her heart safe in the hands of the man who had captured her very essence and claimed it as his own. And with each passing day, she found herself falling deeper and deeper in love with Surya, knowing that their bond was unbreakable, their love eternal.

In the intimate embrace of their love, Lily and Surya found themselves lost in a world of ecstasy and euphoria, where time seemed to stand still and all their worries faded into insignificance. With each tender caress and lingering kiss, they embarked on a journey of passion and intimacy, their bodies entwined in a dance of desire and longing.

As their love making unfolded, the air was filled with a symphony of sighs and whispers, each breath a testament to the intensity of their connection. With every touch, they explored new depths of pleasure, their souls entangled in a web of shared desire and unspoken longing.

In the soft glow of moonlight filtering through the curtains, they surrendered themselves completely to the moment, their bodies moving in perfect harmony as they reached new heights of bliss. Each kiss was a promise of devotion, each caress a declaration of undying love, as they poured their hearts and souls into the act of love making.

Their union was a celebration of their love, a sacred bond forged in the flames of desire and tempered by the trials of life. In each other's arms, they found solace and fulfillment, their love transcending the physical realm and reaching towards the heavens.

And as they lay tangled together in the afterglow of their passion, their hearts soared with joy and contentment, knowing that they had found true happiness in each other's arms. For in that moment, they were not just lovers, but soulmates, bound together for eternity by the power of their love. As Lily and Surya wandered through the vibrant streets of Indore, their hands intertwined like two souls bound together by fate. With each step they took, Surya eagerly showed Lily his favorite spots in the city, pointing out hidden gems and beloved landmarks that held a special place in his heart.

Their exploration led them to bustling markets filled with colorful fabrics and exotic spices, where the aroma of street food wafted through the air, tantalizing their senses. Surya delighted in introducing Lily to the culinary delights of Indore, urging her to sample local delicacies and traditional dishes that he had grown up enjoying.

With each bite, Lily experienced a new world of flavors and textures, her taste buds tingling with excitement as she savored the unique blend of spices and ingredients that characterized Indore's cuisine. From spicy street snacks to hearty home-cooked meals, Surya made sure that Lily got a taste of everything that the city had to offer.

As they roamed the streets hand in hand, their laughter mingling with the sounds of the city, Lily felt a deep sense of belonging and contentment. In Surya's company, Indore felt like home, and she knew that she had found a kindred spirit who would always be by her side, guiding her through life's adventures with love and laughter.

As they laughed, talked, and explored the city hand in hand, Lily and Surya's love only grew deeper, reaffirming their commitment to each other with each passing day. Despite the challenges they faced and the miles that separated them, their love remained unwavering, a beacon of hope and strength that guided them through every trial and triumph they encountered on their journey together.

♡♡♡

12

For a moment I lost you

As the new year approached, Lily and Surya had excitedly planned a trip to Ooty, nestled in the lap of the Nilgiri Mountains in southern India, Ooty, also known as Udhagamandalam, is a serene hill station that captivates visitors with its lush greenery, misty landscapes, and pleasant climate. Famous for its tea gardens, winding roads, and colonial charm, Ooty offers a perfect escape from the hustle and bustle of city life. Visitors can explore the picturesque Ooty Lake, take a ride on the historic Nilgiri Mountain Railway, or wander through the vibrant flower gardens. Adventure enthusiasts can trek through the dense forests of the Western Ghats or indulge in outdoor activities like boating and horse riding. With its tranquil ambiance and breathtaking vistas, Ooty truly enchants travelers seeking solace in nature's embrace. A picturesque hill station known for its scenic beauty and chilly climate. They looked forward to welcoming the new year together amidst the serene surroundings of the mountains.

As Lily and Surya arrived in Ooty, the air was crisp with anticipation, their hearts brimming with excitement at the prospect of exploring the picturesque hill station together. After checking into their hotel and freshening up, they embarked on their sightseeing adventure, eager to immerse themselves in the beauty of Ooty's landscapes.

Yet, amidst the breathtaking vistas and idyllic surroundings, a shadow of discord began to loom over their day. What started as a simple disagreement quickly escalated into a heated argument, fueled by misunderstandings and unspoken tensions that simmered beneath the surface.

Lily's heart sank as she found herself locked in a battle of words with Surya, the harsh tones of their voices punctuating the serene tranquility of their surroundings. Emotions ran high as frustrations mounted, each word spoken cutting deeper than the last.

In the heat of the moment, accusations were hurled and wounds were reopened, leaving Lily and Surya reeling in the aftermath of their confrontation. The once-promising day had devolved into a battlefield of emotions, leaving them both wounded and bewildered by the sudden turn of events.

However, their anticipation turned to disappointment as their trip took an unexpected turn. What was meant to be a joyful getaway soon became overshadowed by tension and conflict.

Lily's revelation about her past with Adi came as a shock to Surya. He couldn't understand why Lily had kept this from him, why she hadn't been honest about something so significant. As Lily began to explain her history with Adi, Surya's initial shock turned into a whirlwind of emotions: anger, confusion, and hurt.

Lily recounted how she had met Adi during her college years. They were young and reckless, and their relationship was intense but tumultuous. Adi had been charming and charismatic, drawing Lily into his world with promises of adventure and excitement. For a while, Lily was swept up in the whirlwind romance, believing that she had found her soulmate.

But as time passed, cracks began to appear in their relationship. Adi's unpredictable behavior and his tendency to prioritize his own desires over Lily's well-being caused strain and conflict between them. Despite her love for him, Lily knew deep down that their relationship was unhealthy and unsustainable.

Eventually, Lily found the strength to end things with Adi and move on with her life. She focused on her studies and her career, determined to leave her past behind her. When she met Surya, she felt like she had been given a second chance at love a chance to start fresh and build a future with someone who truly cared for her.

However, as she poured her heart out to Surya, recounting the pain and the mistakes of her past, she could see the hurt and betrayal in his eyes. Surya couldn't understand why Lily had kept such an important part of her life hidden from him. He felt like he had been deceived, like he didn't truly know the woman he loved.

Lily felt a pang of guilt as she realized the depth of Surya's pain. She hadn't meant to hurt him, but she could see now that her silence had caused him a great deal of anguish. She knew that she had to make things right, to rebuild the trust that had been broken between them.

The revelation of Lily's past with Adi stirred a storm of emotions within Surya. Anger, hurt, and a profound sense of betrayal surged through him as he grappled with the fact that Lily had kept such a significant part of her life hidden from him. He couldn't shake the feeling that their relationship had been built on a foundation of lies, and the realization left him reeling.

As the truth sank in, Surya's anger boiled over, and he confronted Lily with the full force of his emotions. Their usually calm and harmonious interactions devolved into a heated argument fueled by pent-up frustration and resentment. Words were exchanged like daggers, cutting deep into the core of their relationship.

Surya felt blindsided by Lily's secrecy, questioning himself again whether he truly knew the woman he loved. He couldn't fathom why she had chosen to conceal such an integral part of her past, and the uncertainty gnawed at him. In his mind, trust had been shattered, and the foundation of their relationship felt unstable beneath his feet.

Lily, in turn, was overwhelmed by Surya's reaction. She hadn't anticipated the depth of his anger and hurt, and seeing the pain in his eyes only added to her own sense of guilt and remorse. She tried to explain her reasons for keeping her past hidden, but her words fell on deaf ears as Surya's anger continued to burn unchecked.

Their fight raged on, each accusation and rebuttal fueling the flames of discord between them. It was a painful and exhausting ordeal, leaving both Lily and Surya emotionally drained and raw. In the heat of the moment, it seemed as though their relationship might fracture irreparably under the weight of their unresolved issues.

Unable to see eye to eye, Lily and Surya reached a breaking point, deciding to part ways and end their relationship. The decision to break up weighed heavily on both of them, and as they traveled back to their respective homes alone, a profound sense of sadness and regret washed over them.

Alone with her thoughts, Lily couldn't hold back the tears that flowed freely down her cheeks. The pain of their separation was palpable, and she couldn't shake the feeling of emptiness that consumed her heart. She mourned the loss of what they once shared, grappling with the realization that their love story had come to an abrupt and painful end.

Despite the distance between them, Surya's heart also ached with sorrow. The echoes of their arguments lingered in his mind, and he found himself questioning whether they had made the right decision. Doubt gnawed at him, and he couldn't shake the feeling that he had let go of something truly precious.

In the silence of their solitude, both Lily and Surya wrestled with their emotions, grappling with the aftermath of their breakup and coming to terms with the reality of their newfound separation. The road ahead seemed uncertain and daunting, filled with the echoes of what could have been and the painful sting of what was lost.

Yet, amidst the darkness of their despair, a glimmer of hope remained. Despite the pain of their parting, the love they once shared still lingered within their hearts, a beacon of light in the midst of their darkest hour. And though they traveled separate paths for now, the possibility of reconciliation lingered on the horizon, a flicker of hope amidst the shadows of their broken dreams.

In the quiet solitude of her room, Lily sat down with pen in hand, her heart heavy with the weight of unspoken words and unresolved emotions. With trembling fingers, she began to pour her soul onto the blank pages before her, each word a testament to the love that still lingered in the depths of her heart.

Dear Surya,

I find myself at a loss for words as I sit down to write this letter, my heart heavy with the weight of unspoken emotions and unshed tears. There are so many things I want to say to you, so many feelings I wish I could express, and yet the words seem to elude me. But I will try my best to put into words what lies heavy on my heart.

First and foremost, I want to thank you. Thank you for the moments we shared, for the laughter and the tears, for the love that we both felt so deeply. From the moment I saw you, I knew that you were someone special, someone who would change my life in ways I could never have imagined. And indeed, you did. You brought joy and happiness into my life, filling each day with light and laughter.

I want to tell you about Adi, my past, and the mistakes I made in keeping it from you. I understand if this comes as a shock, and I am truly sorry for not being honest with you from the beginning. Please know that I never meant to hurt you or deceive you in any way.

Adi was a part of my life before I met you, and though our relationship is now in the past, I realize that I should have been upfront with you about it. I should have trusted you enough to share my history with you, and for that, I am deeply sorry.

I understand if this news upsets you, if it makes you question our relationship and the trust between us. I can only hope that you can find it in your heart to forgive me, to understand that I am only human and that I make mistakes just like everyone else.

I cherish every moment we spent together, from the early days of our friendship to the bittersweet end of our journey. Every text message, every phone call, every shared smile and stolen glance – they are all precious memories that I will hold dear to my heart. I remember the first time you texted me, the first time we spoke on the phone, the first time we met in person – each moment etched into my mind like a beautiful melody that I never want to forget.

Our wedding in Instagram, though unconventional, remains one of the happiest days of my life. The thought of being your wife filled me with a sense of joy and fulfillment that I had never known before. You accepted me completely, flaws and all, and for that, I will be forever grateful. Our time together was filled with love and laughter, with shared dreams and whispered promises. I will always treasure those memories, no matter where life may take us.

But as much as I cherish the moments we shared, I also acknowledge the mistakes I made, the lies I told, and the trust I betrayed. I was scared, Surya – scared of losing you, scared of facing the truth, scared of being alone. And in my fear, I made choices that I now regret. I hurt you, and for that, I am truly sorry. I understand now that love is not about possession or control, but about trust and honesty. I failed you in that regard, and for that, I am truly sorry.

I know that I am not perfect, Surya. I am flawed and imperfect, with a past that haunts me and a future that terrifies me. But through it all, one thing remains constant – my love for you. It burns brightly in the depths of my soul, a flame that refuses to be extinguished. And though we may be apart now, know that you will always have a piece of my heart with you, wherever you may go.

I cannot promise to be perfect, Surya, but I can promise to love you with all that I am, for as long as I live. I can promise to cherish the memories we shared and to hold onto them tightly, even as we walk separate paths. And most importantly, I can promise to never stop fighting for us, for the love that binds us together, for the hope that one day, we will find our way back to each other.

I am grateful for every moment we shared, for every laugh, every tear, every whispered word of affection. You have been a guiding light in the darkness, a beacon of hope and love that I never knew I needed until you came into my life. For that, I will always be thankful.

Despite the pain of our parting, I still believe that you are the best person I have ever met. Your kindness, your compassion, your unwavering support - these are qualities that I will always cherish and hold dear. You were, and will always be, the best man in my eyes.

But now, as I navigate the stormy seas of my emotions, I realize that I must let go of the fairy tale dreams and face the harsh reality of my nightmares. It hurts to admit it, but perhaps our love was nothing more than a beautiful illusion, a fleeting moment of happiness in a sea of sadness and despair.

And so, I will cry and cry until my tears form an ocean, until my heartache becomes a distant memory, until I am able to find peace within myself once more. But know this, Surya - the sea within me may be deep, but it will never drown me. I am stronger than I know, and I will emerge from this darkness with a renewed sense of purpose and determination.

Thank you for everything, Surya. Though our paths may have diverged, know that you will always hold a special place in my heart.

With all my love,

Lily

As Lily sat at her desk, fingers trembling over the keys of her laptop, tears blurred her vision, threatening to spill onto the screen below. With each keystroke, her heartache poured out in the form of words, a desperate attempt to convey the turmoil raging within her soul.

With a heavy sigh, she clicked on the "Send" button, her heart wrenching with the weight of her decision. As the email vanished into the digital abyss, a sense of finality washed over her, leaving her feeling utterly alone in the darkness of her room.

With a soft sob, Lily buried her face in her hands, the sound of her tears echoing in the silence of the night. Every fiber of her being ached with the pain of loss and regret, her chest constricted with the weight of unspoken emotions.

In the solitude of her room, surrounded by shadows and memories, Lily allowed herself to grieve for what could have been. Her tears flowed freely, a silent testament to the depth of her anguish and the magnitude of her sorrow.

Hours passed in a blur of misery and despair, the darkness of the night enveloping her like a shroud. And as the first light of dawn crept through the window, casting a pale glow upon her tear-stained cheeks, Lily knew that the road ahead would be long and fraught with uncertainty.

The days stretched on, marked by an eerie silence between Lily and Surya. What had once been a vibrant connection between them now lay dormant, suffocated by the weight of their unresolved issues. With each passing moment, the distance between them grew wider, both physically and emotionally.

Communication dwindled to nothing, replaced by a void of silence that echoed with the echoes of their unspoken words. Messages remained unsent, calls unmade, as Lily and Surya retreated into their separate worlds, nursing wounds that refused to heal.

Longing lingered in the air, a palpable ache that underscored their shared absence. Lily found herself yearning for Surya's presence, his voice, his touch, yet unable to bridge the chasm that had opened up between them. Meanwhile, Surya grappled with his own turmoil, wrestling with feelings of betrayal and hurt that seemed to grow more insurmountable with each passing day.

The silence weighed heavy on them both, a suffocating blanket of unspoken truths and unresolved emotions. They moved through their days with a sense of emptiness, the absence of each other's presence a constant reminder of what they had lost.

Yet even in the midst of their silence, a flicker of hope remained a tiny ember of the love that had once burned bright between them. It was a fragile flame, easily extinguished by the winds of doubt and fear, but still, it persisted, casting a faint glow in the darkness of their separation.

As the days turned into weeks, Lily and Surya found themselves at a crossroads, faced with the choice of either letting their silence consume them or finding the courage to confront their demons and seek reconciliation. It was a daunting prospect, fraught with uncertainty and pain, but deep down, they both knew that they couldn't bear to lose each other forever.

On that fateful day, the weight of silence was shattered by the ringing of Lily's phone. With trembling hands, she answered, her heart pounding with anticipation. It was Surya the sound of his voice breaking through the barriers of their silence like a ray of sunlight piercing through storm clouds.

"Surya?" Lily's voice quivered, a mixture of hope and apprehension.

"Lily," came Surya's gentle reply, filled with emotion. "I'm sorry. I'm so, so sorry. I didn't understand. I didn't see what was right in front of me."

Tears welled up in Lily's eyes as she listened to the raw vulnerability in Surya's voice. It was as if a dam had burst, unleashing a torrent of pent-up emotions that had been brewing beneath the surface for far too long.

"Surya, I..." Lily's voice caught in her throat, choked with emotion. "I missed you so much."

Surya's response was immediate, his words tumbling out in a rush of confession and longing. "Lily, I can't live without you. Every day without you feels like an eternity. I miss you more than words can say."

The floodgates opened then, as Lily and Surya poured out their hearts to each other, laying bare their deepest fears and regrets. They spoke of the pain of their separation, the loneliness that had gnawed at their souls, and the overwhelming love that still burned bright within them.

Tears mingled with laughter as they reminisced about happier times, their voices growing stronger with each shared memory. And as the minutes stretched into hours, it was as if time itself had ceased to exist, leaving only the warmth of their connection to fill the void between them.

In that moment of reconciliation, Lily and Surya found solace in each other's arms, their tears of sorrow transforming into tears of joy. And as they whispered words of love and forgiveness, they knew that no matter what challenges lay ahead, they would face them together, united in their unwavering devotion to each other.

ᖾᖾᖾ

13

Taking Our Relationship to the Next Level

As the festive lights of Diwali illuminated their surroundings, Surya's heart swelled with anticipation. This year's celebration held a significance beyond the usual pomp and splendor: it was a moment he had been eagerly awaiting, a moment to introduce Lily to his family and pave the way for their future together.

With a nervous yet determined resolve, Surya broached the topic with Lily, his words infused with excitement and hope. "Lily, I want to share something with you," he began, his voice tinged with anticipation. "I want to introduce you to my family this Diwali. I want them to know about us, about you."

Lily's eyes widened with surprise, her heart skipping a beat at the thought of meeting Surya's family. "Really?" she exclaimed; her voice laced with excitement. "I would love that!"

In the days leading up to Diwali, Surya meticulously planned every detail of their meeting, rehearsing what he would say and imagining the reactions of his family members. And when the auspicious day finally arrived, he stood before his loved ones with Lily by his side, his heart brimming with pride.

Taking a deep breath, Surya gathered his courage and addressed his family, his words filled with conviction and sincerity. "This is Lily," he began, his voice steady despite the flutter of nerves in his stomach. "She's the one I want to spend the rest of my life with. She's kind, she's loving, and she's everything I've ever dreamed of."

With a warm smile, Surya shared stories of their time together, painting a vivid picture of Lily's personality and character. He showed them photos of Lily, each image capturing a precious moment they had shared, and watched as his family's expressions softened with approval.

To Surya's relief and delight, his family welcomed Lily with open arms, embracing her as one of their own. They showered her with affection and blessings, expressing their happiness at the prospect of her joining their family.

As the evening unfolded, Lily felt a sense of belonging wash over her, surrounded by the warmth and acceptance of Surya's loved ones. And as she exchanged smiles and laughter with his family members, she knew in her heart that this Diwali would mark the beginning of a new chapter in their lives a chapter filled with love, joy, and the promise of a future together.

The joyous celebration with Surya's family brought a new wave of apprehension for Lily. While she basked in the warmth of acceptance from Surya's loved ones, her thoughts were consumed by the daunting task that lay ahead telling her own parents about their relationship.

As the days passed and the echoes of Diwali faded, Lily found herself grappling with a sense of unease. The prospect of revealing her relationship with Surya to her parents loomed over her like a dark cloud, casting a shadow of uncertainty over their otherwise blissful union.

Surya, sensing Lily's inner turmoil, offered his unwavering support and reassurance. "We'll face this together, Lily," he would say, his voice infused with quiet determination. "Whatever happens, I'll be by your side."

But despite Surya's comforting words, Lily couldn't shake the nagging fear that gnawed at her heart. The thought of disappointing her parents, of facing their disapproval, filled her with a deep sense of dread. She agonized over the potential consequences of revealing their relationship the arguments, the misunderstandings, the rift it might create within her family.

With each passing day, Lily found herself retreating further into silence, unable to muster the courage to broach the subject with her parents. The weight of her secret became a heavy burden, threatening to suffocate her with its oppressive presence.

Yet beneath her fear and apprehension, a glimmer of hope flickered a hope that perhaps, in time, her parents would come to understand and accept her love for Surya. It was a fragile hope, but one that she clung to tenaciously, like a lifeline in the darkness.

As the days turned into weeks and the weeks into months, Lily wrestled with her inner turmoil, caught between the desire to protect her family and the longing to embrace her own happiness.

Surya's commitment to their relationship shone brightly through his unwavering determination to facilitate their future together. With each passing day, he tirelessly pursued the possibility of transferring to Indore, knowing that it held the key to their happiness.

For Lily, Surya's efforts were a beacon of hope in the midst of her uncertainty. She found solace in the knowledge that he was working tirelessly to bridge the gap between them, both physically and emotionally. Yet, the burden of secrecy weighed heavily on her heart, casting a shadow over their otherwise promising future.

As they waited for news of Surya's transfer, Lily grappled with conflicting emotions. On one hand, she longed to share the joy of their relationship with her parents, to bask in the warmth of their approval and support. On the other hand, she feared the repercussions of revealing their love a fear that threatened to consume her with its relentless intensity.

Amidst the backdrop of their blossoming careers and burgeoning love, the shadows of familial expectations loomed large, casting a pall over Surya and Lily's relationship. Their differing family backgrounds and the divergent paths they had walked threatened to sow seeds of discord between them, leading to misunderstandings and tensions that tested the strength of their bond.

As Lily soared to new heights in her career, her achievements served as a testament to her dedication and resilience. Yet, with each milestone she reached, the gap between her aspirations and her family's expectations widened, adding fuel to the simmering conflict between tradition and independence.

For Surya, the pressures of familial duty weighed heavily on his shoulders, as he grappled with the conflicting desires of his heart and the expectations placed upon him by his family. Caught between loyalty to his loved ones and his unwavering devotion to Lily, he found himself torn between two worlds, struggling to find a balance that would satisfy both his family and his beloved.

In the midst of these external pressures, Surya and Lily's relationship bore the brunt of their internal conflicts. Small misunderstandings snowballed into heated arguments, fueled by the underlying tension that simmered beneath the surface. Yet, even in their moments of discord, their love remained a guiding light, a beacon of hope that illuminated the darkness and guided them through the storm.

As they navigated the turbulent waters of their relationship, Surya and Lily learned valuable lessons about communication, compromise, and the true meaning of love. Through their trials and tribulations, they emerged stronger and more resilient, their bond forged in the fires of adversity.

The news of Surya's transfer to Indore, a glimmer of hope pierced through the clouds of uncertainty that had shrouded Lily and Surya's relationship. For the first time in what felt like an eternity, the prospect of being together, of waking up to each other's smiles and sharing their lives without the barrier of distance, seemed within reach.

Lily's heart swelled with joy at the news, her spirits lifted by the promise of reuniting with Surya after what felt like an eternity apart. The thought of having him by her side, of being able to reach out and touch him, filled her with a sense of warmth and contentment that she had sorely missed.

After enduring months of separation and longing, their long-distance relationship was finally drawing to a close. No more endless nights spent yearning for each other's presence, no more fleeting moments stolen through phone calls and video chats. Now, they could finally bask in the simple pleasures of togetherness, of sharing their lives in the same physical space.

As Lily eagerly counted down the days until Surya's arrival, she found herself filled with a renewed sense of hope and optimism for their future. The trials and tribulations they had faced had only served to strengthen their bond, reaffirming the depth of their love and commitment to each other.

A new chapter in their love story was about to unfold one filled with endless possibilities, shared dreams, and the promise of a lifetime of happiness together. And as they prepared to embark on this new journey, Lily knew in her heart that their love would only continue to grow stronger with each passing day, transcending the barriers of time and distance to unite them in a bond that was truly unbreakable.

After Surya's transfer to Indore, Lily felt it was the right time to open up to her parents about their relationship. With a mix of anxiety and hope, she journeyed back to her hometown, her mind swirling with thoughts about how her parents would react. She wondered if they would accept Surya and support their relationship, or if they would have reservations. Lily was hopeful for their understanding but also apprehensive about potential challenges they might face. Despite her nerves, she was determined to have this important conversation and share her feelings with her family.

14

Homecoming Conversations: Lily's Big News

After reaching home, Lily gathered her parents together for an important conversation. Lily's heart sank as she poured her heart out to her parents, hoping they would understand her love for Surya and accept their relationship. But instead of warmth and acceptance, she was met with icy disapproval and stern reprimands. Her parents' reaction was like a dagger to her heart, tearing through her hopes and dreams with each harsh word.

She tried to explain, to make them see Surya through her eyes to see the kind, caring man she had fallen deeply in love with. But her pleas fell on deaf ears, drowned out by their rigid beliefs and unfounded prejudices. They were fixated on finding a "better" match for her, someone more suitable in their eyes, someone who ticked all the boxes of societal norms and expectations.

Their words cut deep, leaving Lily feeling helpless and alone, caught between the love she felt for Surya and the expectations of her family. She felt like she was being torn apart, forced to choose between her heart and her family's wishes a choice no one should ever have to make.

As her parents' anger escalated into a full-blown confrontation, Lily felt a wave of despair wash over her. She had hoped they would understand, hoped they would see the happiness Surya brought into her life. But now, faced with their unwavering opposition, she felt lost and defeated, unsure of what the future held for her and Surya.

As Lily's parents delivered their ultimatum, the weight of their words settled heavily on her shoulders, crushing her hopes and dreams beneath their oppressive demands. The choice laid out before her was stark and unforgiving: forsake her love for Surya and remain within the confines of her family's expectations, or follow her heart and face the prospect of exile from everything she had ever known.

Tears streamed down Lily's cheeks as she pleaded with her parents, her voice trembling with desperation and anguish. She begged them to reconsider, to open their hearts to the possibility of her happiness with Surya. She recounted their moments together, the love they shared, the dreams they had woven together. But her parents remained unmoved, their resolve unyielding in the face of her entreaties.

With each rejection, Lily's heart shattered a little more, the pain of losing her family's acceptance driving a wedge between her and the life she had once known. She was torn between her loyalty to her parents and her love for Surya, torn between the familiar comforts of home and the uncertain path that lay ahead.

As Lily's tears flowed unchecked, her pleas for understanding fell on deaf ears, her parents unmoved by her distress. Despite her heartfelt appeals and the raw emotion etched across her face, their resolve remained unshaken, their hearts hardened against the love that had blossomed between Lily and Surya.

Each tear that fell from Lily's eyes seemed to echo the weight of her despair, a silent testament to the depth of her anguish. She begged and pleaded with her parents, her voice cracking with emotion, her words choked with sorrow. But their hearts remained closed to her pain, their minds made up, unwavering in their decision to reject her love.

With each rejection, Lily's hope dimmed, her dreams of a future with Surya slipping further from her grasp. She felt the crushing weight of their disapproval pressing down upon her, suffocating her spirit, leaving her gasping for breath in the suffocating grip of their expectations.

Yet even in the depths of her despair, Lily refused to surrender to defeat. She continued to fight, to cling to the fragile hope that somehow, someway, she could bridge the divide between her love for Surya and her duty to her family. But as her parents remained resolute in their decision, their hearts unmoved by her tears, Lily knew that her battle had been lost before it had even begun.

As Lily's mind swirled with memories of past traumas and present struggles, she found herself confronted with the harsh reality of her situation. The echoes of her tumultuous childhood, marred by domestic violence and betrayal, reverberated through her thoughts, casting a shadow over her present predicament.

Yet amidst the chaos of her emotions, a beacon of light emerged: Surya's unwavering support and steadfast care. In him, she found solace, strength, and an unwavering ally in the face of adversity. His presence was a constant reminder that she was not alone, that she had someone by her side who would stand by her through thick and thin.

With each passing moment, Lily's resolve grew stronger, her determination to forge her own path unyielding. She realized that she could no longer allow herself to be bound by the constraints of familial expectations, that her happiness and well-being mattered more than conforming to the wishes of others.

And so, with a heart heavy with the weight of her decision yet buoyed by the promise of a future with Surya, Lily made her choice. She would leave behind the familiar comforts of home, the echoes of her parents' disapproval fading into the background as she set her sights on a new beginning, a life built on love, trust, and mutual respect.

Though the road ahead was fraught with uncertainty and challenges, Lily knew that she was making the right decision for herself. She would marry Surya, not out of defiance or rebellion, but out of a deep-seated conviction that their love was worth fighting for, that together, they could overcome any obstacle that stood in their way.

But in the depths of her despair, Lily found a flicker of courage, a glimmer of determination to forge her own destiny, even if it meant sacrificing the ties that bound her to her family. With a heavy heart and tear-streaked face, she made her decision to stand by Surya, to choose love over duty, even if it meant walking away from everything she had ever known.

With a heavy heart and a soul weighed down by grief, Lily accepted the harsh reality of her situation. She understood that she could not force her parents to accept her choices, that their love came with conditions she could not bear to meet. And so, with a final, tearful goodbye, Lily turned her back on the home she had known, the echoes of her parents' rejection ringing in her ears as she walked away, her heart heavy with the burden of lost love and shattered dreams.

In the midst of Lily's turmoil, she found solace in the unwavering support of Surya. As she poured out her heart to him, sharing her deepest fears and insecurities, he listened with compassion and understanding, offering her the reassurance she so desperately needed.

With unwavering conviction, Surya vowed to stand by Lily's side, to be her rock and her anchor in the storm. He promised to marry her, to protect her, and to cherish her for all eternity. His words, filled with sincerity and love, instilled in Lily a newfound sense of hope and security.

As she gazed into his eyes, she saw not only the depth of his devotion but also the unwavering strength of their bond. In that moment, she knew without a doubt that she could trust him with her heart, that he would never lead her astray or betray her trust.

With Surya by her side, Lily felt a sense of peace wash over her, knowing that together they could weather any storm. In his arms, she found the strength to face the challenges ahead, secure in the knowledge that their love would guide them through even the darkest of times.

And so, with Surya's unwavering support and steadfast commitment, Lily took her first steps towards a future filled with love, hope, and endless possibilities. With him by her side, she knew that she could overcome any obstacle that stood in their way, for their love was a force stronger than any adversity.

Amidst Lily's heartache and the rejection, she faced at her family home, a ray of solace emerged from an unexpected source - Surya and his family. Understanding Lily's predicament, they stood firmly by her side, offering unwavering support and reassurance during her time of need. With empathy and understanding, Surya's family extended their comforting embrace to Lily, assuring her that everything would eventually fall into place. Despite the initial turmoil, the warmth and acceptance from Surya's family served as a beacon of hope, infusing Lily's heart with newfound courage and determination. Moved by their kindness, Lily found solace in the midst of uncertainty, knowing that she had found a second family in Surya's loving embrace. United by their shared love and unwavering support, Surya and Lily embarked on a journey towards their wedding day, strengthened by the bonds of love and kinship that transcended all barriers.

In the heart of Indore, amidst the vibrant colors and joyous celebrations of an Indian Hindu wedding, Lily and Surya embarked on a journey that would bind their souls together for eternity. The air was filled with the sweet fragrance of jasmine flowers, and the sound of traditional music echoed through the halls, setting the stage for a celebration unlike any other.

15

The Last Love's Embrace

On the auspicious day of their marriage, the air was filled with palpable excitement and anticipation, as Surya and Lily prepared to embark on the next chapter of their lives together. The venue adorned with vibrant hues and fragrant blooms, echoed with the joyous laughter of friends and family, who had gathered to celebrate the union of two souls deeply in love. As the sun dipped below the horizon, casting a warm glow upon the ceremony.

As the auspicious hour approached, Lily, adorned in the resplendent hues of a crimson saree adorned with intricate gold embroidery, awaited her beloved with bated breath. Her eyes sparkled with anticipation, and her heart fluttered with excitement as she prepared to take the sacred vows of marriage.

Meanwhile, Surya, dressed in the regal attire of a traditional sherwani, stood tall and proud, his gaze fixed on the entrance where his beloved would soon make her grand entrance. His heart swelled with love and anticipation, knowing that soon he would be united with the woman who had captured his heart.

As the ceremonial rituals began, the priest chanted ancient mantras invoking the blessings of the gods upon the union of Lily and Surya. Amidst the fragrance of incense and the gentle glow of flickering candles, the couple exchanged floral garlands, symbolizing their acceptance and mutual respect for one another.

Next came the sacred ceremony of the mangal phera, where Lily and Surya walked around the sacred fire seven times, each round representing a vow they made to each other. With each step, they pledged their love, devotion, and unwavering commitment to one another, promising to stand by each other's side through all of life's trials and triumphs.

As the ceremony reached its crescendo, Lily and Surya exchanged vows and garlands, sealing their union with a sacred knot known as the mangalsutra. Amidst the joyful cheers and blessings of their loved ones, they were pronounced husband and wife, embarking on a journey of love, companionship, and shared destiny.

The wedding festivities continued late into the night, with sumptuous feasts, lively music, and joyous dancing. Friends and family came together to celebrate the union of two souls destined to be together, showering Lily and Surya with blessings, love, and good wishes for their future together.

As the stars twinkled overhead and the sounds of laughter and merriment filled the air, Lily and Surya reveled in the joy of their newfound union, grateful for the love that had brought them together and the promise of a lifetime of happiness that lay ahead.

In the gentle embrace of their enduring love, Lily and Surya's life blossomed into a wondrous journey of happiness and fulfillment. With each passing day, their bond grew stronger, weathering every storm and basking in the warmth of their unwavering commitment to each other.

Lily and Surya embarked on a journey filled with shared adventures and cherished moments. Their married life became a tapestry woven with threads of love, trust, and companionship.

Together, they traversed the winding paths of life, exploring new destinations and creating lasting memories. From the bustling streets of metropolitan cities to the serene landscapes of quaint countryside, Lily and Surya immersed themselves in the beauty of the world around them. Each journey brought them closer together, strengthening their bond as they navigated the ups and downs of life hand in hand.

Amidst the adventures, they also faced challenges that tested their resilience and commitment to each other. But through every obstacle, Lily and Surya stood united, drawing strength from their unwavering love and unwavering support for one another.

Their married life was not just about the grand adventures and thrilling escapades; it was also about the simple moments of togetherness and intimacy. Whether sharing quiet evenings at home or stealing fleeting glances across crowded rooms, Lily and Surya found solace in each other's presence, knowing that they were each other's rock in a tumultuous world.

As they celebrated their second anniversary, Lily and Surya reflected on the journey they had undertaken together, grateful for the love that had bound them together and excited for the adventures that lay ahead. Theirs was a love that had grown stronger with time, a love that had weathered storms and emerged even more resilient. And as they looked towards the future, they did so with hearts full of hope and anticipation, knowing that their love would continue to guide them through whatever life had in store.

From the moment they discovered they were expecting, Surya made it his priority to cater to Lily's every need. He took on household chores with enthusiasm, sparing Lily the physical strain and ensuring she could rest and relax. Whether it was cooking her favorite meals or tidying up the house, Surya handled everything with care and attention to detail.

During Lily's pregnancy, Surya assumed the role of caretaker with utmost dedication and tenderness. He approached this new responsibility with a deep sense of love and devotion, ensuring that Lily felt supported and cherished every step of the way.

As Lily's pregnancy progressed, Surya became increasingly attentive to her well-being. He accompanied her to doctor's appointments, holding her hand during check-ups and eagerly listening to updates about their unborn child. Surya made sure Lily followed her doctor's advice, reminding her to take her prenatal vitamins and stay hydrated.

Emotionally, Surya was Lily's pillar of strength. He listened patiently to her concerns and fears, offering words of reassurance and comfort whenever she needed them. Surya made sure to pamper Lily, showering her with affection and affectionate gestures to remind her of how cherished she was.

During the more challenging moments of pregnancy, such as morning sickness or mood swings, Surya remained steadfast in his support. He remained by Lily's side, offering soothing words and gentle caresses to ease her discomfort. Surya never faltered in his commitment to being there for Lily, understanding that his unwavering presence was essential to her peace of mind.

Above all, Surya embraced the role of caregiver with unwavering love and devotion, cherishing every moment of this precious journey with Lily. He understood the significance of this chapter in their lives and was determined to make it as smooth and memorable as possible for his beloved wife.

As the time for delivery drew near, Surya's anticipation and excitement reached new heights. He ensured that everything was meticulously prepared for the arrival of their little one, from packing the hospital bag to setting up the nursery at home. Surya made sure that Lily felt calm and reassured, constantly reminding her of his unwavering support and love.

When the day finally arrived, Surya stood by Lily's side, holding her hand tightly as they made their way to the hospital. He remained a constant source of strength and encouragement throughout the labor process, offering words of comfort and motivation during each contraction.

Inside the delivery room, Surya remained a pillar of support for Lily, providing physical and emotional assistance every step of the way. He held her hand, wiped her brow, and whispered words of encouragement as she bravely faced the challenges of childbirth.

ᑭᑭᑭ

16

Welcoming Our Little Miracle

As their precious baby entered the world, Surya's heart swelled with overwhelming joy and gratitude. Tears of happiness welled up in his eyes as he witnessed the miracle of birth, feeling an indescribable sense of awe and wonder at the sight of their newborn child.

In the moments that followed, Surya remained by Lily's side, cherishing the first precious moments with their baby. He held their newborn daughter in his arms, marveling at her tiny features and feeling an overwhelming sense of love and protectiveness wash over him.

Throughout the entire delivery process, Surya's unwavering love and support never wavered. He remained a steadfast presence for Lily, ensuring that she felt safe, loved, and supported every step of the way. Together, they welcomed their bundle of joy into the world, embarking on a new chapter of their lives filled with boundless love and happiness.

Their home was graced with the arrival of a precious gift a baby girl they lovingly named Jiyaa. With her arrival, their lives were forever transformed, filled with boundless joy and endless possibilities. Jiyaa became the living embodiment of their love, her laughter echoing through the halls of their home, filling every corner with a sense of pure happiness.

Surya and Lily's journey, fraught with challenges and joys, culminated in the birth of their daughter, Jiyaa. Holding their newborn in their arms, they felt a profound sense of completeness and contentment. As they looked into Jiyaa's eyes, they saw reflections of their love, resilience, and unwavering commitment to each other. With Jiyaa as their beacon of hope and happiness, they embraced their future with renewed vigor and an unbreakable bond, knowing that their love would continue to flourish and grow stronger with each passing day.

As Jiyaa grew, she became the center of their universe, her innocent giggles and curious eyes bringing light and laughter into their lives. Lily and Surya watched in awe as their daughter discovered the world around her, her every milestone a testament to the beauty of life and the miracle of parenthood.

Together, as a family, they shared countless precious moments – from tender bedtime stories to playful games in the park. Lily and Surya cherished every second spent with their darling daughter, her presence a constant reminder of the love and joy that filled their hearts.

With Jiyaa by their side, Lily and Surya's love story took on a new dimension, enriched by the laughter and innocence of their beloved daughter. As they looked into her eyes, they saw the reflection of their love: a love that had endured the test of time and had blossomed into something truly beautiful.

And so, surrounded by the boundless love of their daughter, Lily and Surya lived their lives happily ever after, their hearts overflowing with gratitude for the precious gift of family and the enduring power of love.

ৡৡৡ

"In the garden of my heart, you are the eternal sunshine that blooms every day, scattering the darkness with your radiant warmth"

"Thank you for reading my book. Have a happy day."